"I wan

"You're going to have to prove he's your baby first," Grady said.

"I'm not leaving here without him."

Grady looked at Jenna's mouth, which was damp and soft. He wanted to drag her into his arms and kiss her again, reason be damned. He wanted to take her to his bed and make wild passionate love to her again, and then deal with this mess. But that was impossible.

"Or if you'd rather," she said, "I'll stay here and help you take care of Andy until we get the results of the blood tests back."

"No," Grady said.

"Don't do this to me," she whispered. "Don't take my baby from me."

Dear Reader,

What happens when a baby is found on a doorstep and three very different men each become convinced that *he* is the true father of the cute, cooing infant?

You're about to meet the third of these wonderfully special single dads. After all, Grady Nolan has every reason to believe *he* fathered the baby on the doorstep!

We hope you'll enjoy the hunt for the parents of the baby on the doorstep!

Regards,

Debra Matteucci
Senior Editor and Editorial Coordinator

Cathy Gillen Thacker

TOO MANY MOMS

Harlequin Books

TORONTO • NEW YORK • LONDON
AMSTERDAM • PARIS • SYDNEY • HAMBURG
STOCKHOLM • ATHENS • TOKYO • MILAN
MADRID • WARSAW • BUDAPEST • AUCKLAND

ISBN 0-373-16529-3

TOO MANY MOMS

This edition published by arrangement with Harlequin Enterprises B. V.

Printed in U.S.A.

Prologue

The phone was ringing when Grady Noland let himself into his apartment. He set his bags down next to the door and propped his skis against the wall. Figuring it was the Philadelphia police department wanting him to come back to work a day early, he grabbed the phone in the kitchen and spoke in a tone that was all business. "Grady here."

"Hey, Grady," Jack Rourke greeted him amiably, an underlying tenseness to his low tone. "I need a favor."

Grady dropped almost two weeks' accumulation of mail on the table and shrugged out of his coat. "Name it," Grady told his friend as he dusted a light covering of snow from his shaggy, sable brown hair and lanky six-foot-four frame.

"Well," Jack sighed, "you're not going to believe this, but . . . a two-month-old baby was left in a heart-shaped red wicker basket decorated with stenciled cupids and a huge white satin bow, on Alec's doorstep, on Valentine's Day."

"Wait a minute. That was over two weeks ago," Grady pointed out with a frown. He pulled a small, leather-bound book from his pocket, picked up a pen and began to make notes as Jack talked.

"Yeah, I know. The first week Alec thought the baby was his," Jack explained.

"And the second week?" Grady asked.

"I thought the baby was mine," Jack said, as if that explained everything. "So I had him."

"Is this for real?" Grady interrupted. The three of them had a history of playing practical jokes on each other.

"You better believe it," Jack said seriously. "And so is the beautiful baby in Rebecca's arms right now."

In the background, Grady could hear a baby gurgling and soft feminine laughter. It did sound like Jack had a woman and a baby with him right now. A happy baby.

"Where are you?" Grady asked.

"Los Angeles," Jack said, "but we're heading back to Philadelphia later this afternoon to see if we can't track down Andy's real parents. Initially, there was a typewritten note left with Baby Andy. It said, and I quote, 'To Andy's father, own up to your mistakes!' "

Grady continued writing. This sounded serious. Like the mother was furious with the baby's father. "Did Alec know who the baby's mother was?" Grady asked.

"Alec thought he did. He thought because of the way the baby was handed over to him, like some fabulous Valentine's Day gift, that Baby Andy was the result of a one-night stand Alec had with a model. It took Alec and the model's sister, Jade Kincaid, a week to find Nicole. When they did, they discovered Nicole wasn't Andy's mother at all, which meant Alec wasn't the father."

"So how did you get involved?" Grady asked with a frown.

"Because Alec called me. This wasn't a random abandonment, Grady, but a well-thought-out ploy to get the baby's father involved in bringing up the baby, and it looked like the mother thought Andy's dad could be reached at Alec's place. Alec had checked his calendar for last year and knew that I had stayed at his house last April while I was gathering background information for a screenplay I was writing."

Grady recalled getting together with Jack while he was in town the previous spring. "That movie about the turn-of-the-century Amish?"

"Right. And while I was there I had what has since turned out to be a lot more than a fling with a beautiful half-English, half-Amish woman. But at the time, I thought a fling was all I was going to ever have with Rebecca."

"And now you know differently?" Grady guessed.

"The lady's just agreed to marry me," Jack said happily.

Grady grinned. "Congratulations!"

"Thanks. Anyway, because Rebecca had no other way to contact me except through Alec, I erroneously assumed the baby left on Alec's doorstep was mine, left out of sheer desperation. And for the last week I've had Andy with me while I tracked Rebecca down, but now I know, as much as we've both come to love Andy, that Andy's not our child, either," Jack continued.

"That's too bad," Grady said as his eye caught a postcard from France sticking out of his stack of mail. He picked it up. It read *Just Married!* on the front, and was signed, "Having a wonderful time, Alec and Jade," on the back. "Hey, is this postcard from Alec for real?" Grady asked disbelievingly. *"Alec's married?"*

"Yeah," Jack confirmed, "he eloped right after he turned Baby Andy over to me. He and I tried to call you, but the department said you'd left town on the fifteenth to go skiing in Sun Valley. We figured the news could wait until you got back from Idaho. They're planning another wedding for family and friends on their return from Europe."

"Wow, that's really great," Grady murmured, still feeling a little stunned to hear Alec had ended his days as one of the country's most sought-after playboys.

"Anyway, Grady," Jack continued, picking up the threads of their conversation, "I was thinking we could start our search by talking to someone in Missing Persons, seeing if any babies have been reported missing in the Philadelphia area."

Grady sighed as his cop's mind went to work on the case. He looked over all the facts he had assembled so far. Abruptly, all the pieces fell into place. Alec and Jack weren't the only ones who'd made reckless love last spring. And anyone who knew Alec, Grady and Jack also knew how close the three of them were, and had been since their college years together at Penn. To get in touch with any one of them, all you had to do was contact one of the three.

"That won't be necessary," Grady said, as the realization hit him with gut-wrenching force. Slowly, he put down his pen and notebook. He had wanted children for a long time, but given up on ever having any of his own. Feeling a little dazed, he said, "I know whose baby this is."

"Don't tell me." Jack paused as the baby continued to coo and gurgle in the background. "You had a fling late last April, too," Jack guessed.

"Two, to be exact," Grady admitted reluctantly as he rubbed the tenseness from the back of his neck. "One was...well, it started during a party at Alec's mansion and ended at my place later that same night."

"And the other?"

Grady groaned aloud as he thought about the possible ramifications there. "Was with my ex-wife."

Chapter One

"Andy is my baby!" Jenna Sullivan proclaimed.

"No," Clarissa Noland stated just as passionately. "He's not. He's my baby."

Grady Noland stared at one beautiful woman, then the other, feeling like he'd walked smack into the middle of a nightmare from which it was impossible to wake up. And then it hit him. The relief he felt was staggering. He relaxed his broad shoulders and flashed them a sexy smile. "I gotta hand it to you," he drawled admiringly. "Alec and Jack have really outdone themselves this time." *They'd really had him going there for a minute. They'd had him completely, utterly buffaloed. But no more.*

"Alec!" Clarissa sputtered indignantly, working hard, Grady thought, to keep up the ruse.

"Jack?" Jenna appeared confused. "What do either of them have to do with this?" Her soft pink bow-shaped lips formed a pout that contrasted nicely with the angelic innocence in her wide, dark green eyes.

Grady frowned. As amusing as this had been, he refused to be played for a fool one instant longer. He tore his distracted gaze from Jenna's creamy complexion and thick, long eyelashes. "The joke's over, ladies," Grady said flatly. He was as amenable to a little mischief as the next guy, but it was time they put *this* farce to bed.

Jenna blinked again, looking completely nonplussed. "What joke?" she asked warily, her soft, throaty voice barely above a whisper.

"C'mon, stop playing games with me," Grady urged impatiently, as he folded his arms in front of him. He had known from the first night he'd met Jenna last spring that she was a damn good sport and a lively companion. Hell, she hadn't even thought twice about stealing a bottle of champagne from Alec's kitchen and ducking out the back door so they could ditch Alec's business-with-pleasure party and walk over to Grady's place. But he'd never figured her for a practical joker, which went to show how much he knew.

"I am not playing games with you," Jenna said, carefully enunciating every word as she took in his squared shoulders and girded thighs.

"Neither am I," Clarissa stormed.

Yeah, right. Grady wished Jenna had worn some other scent. The delicate lavender fragrance was evoking all sorts of erotic memories, none of which it was wise to recall, at least not right now, with his jealous, neurotic ex-wife standing so close by.

Because Jenna seemed the more passionate of the two and the least likely to pull such shenanigans, Grady approached her with a come-on meant to make her cry uncle. "If you want to toy with me, Jenna," Grady drawled sexily as he lifted a hand to tangle in the rich, strawberry blond waves brushing her slender shoulders, "you're going to have to find some other way."

Grady's ex-wife stepped between him and Jenna. "You scoundrel!" Clarissa said.

"I agree," Jenna said to Clarissa. Then she turned to Grady, pushing his hand from her shoulder. "You are a rake and a hellion—"

"Tsk, tsk. Such old-fashioned words." Grady teasingly waggled his eyebrows at Jenna, enjoying the way the color rose in her delicately sculpted cheeks. He stepped even closer. "For such a newfangled prank."

"For the last time, Grady Noland," Jenna ground out between clenched white teeth, her full breasts rising and falling with each aggravated breath she took. "This is not a prank!"

"It has to be," Grady replied confidently. There was no way two women could both truthfully claim to be the mother of his son.

"Only a hopeless bounder like you would think so," Jenna retorted tightly, flushing all the more.

Enjoying the emotion simmering between them, Grady teased, "Give me any more compliments and you'll turn my head."

Jenna ignored his stab at humor. "Not that I should be surprised you've landed me in such a predicament," she said, shaking her head in self-remonstration. "All along I knew you were an irresponsible, no-strings kind of guy."

"Only since his divorce from me," Clarissa said. "Prior to that he was *very* commitment oriented."

"Well, I've changed," Grady said, meaning every word.

"And perhaps not for the better," Jenna muttered.

Her carelessly uttered words hit a nerve. Grady pushed the second thoughts he'd secretly been having about his new life-style away. "Look, you can't both be this baby's mother," he said reasonably. "So this is either the most elaborate practical joke Alec and Jack ever played on me, or—"

"One of us is lying," Jenna finished.

"Right," Grady said uncomfortably, wishing Jenna weren't so damn beautiful. In tight, faded jeans, boots, a long white thigh-skimming sweater and open navy-blue full-length wool coat that made the most of her tall, willowy figure and long lissome legs, she looked sexy. And intriguingly inaccessible.

Clarissa, on the other hand, seemed to have recently gained a little weight. Realizing that made Grady all the more uncomfortable.

Jenna folded her arms in front of her and regarded Grady contentiously.

"Well, as it happens, one of us *is* lying," Clarissa said.

"Yeah, and guess which one," Jenna baited him sarcastically.

Grady always had liked a challenge. Just as he liked Jenna's breezy girl-next-door good looks. She was the kind of woman who'd probably been a varsity cheerleader *and* captain of the debate team in high school, the kind who'd had half the boys in love with her and didn't even know it. Had he gone to high school with Jenna, Grady knew he would have taken one look at her perfect smile, creamy complexion and long-lashed dark green eyes and fallen madly in love with her on the spot. But they weren't in high school anymore.

He released an exasperated breath, shoved his hands through his hair. Apparently, they weren't done with this game, so he figured he might as well play along. "Don't you think I've already tried?"

Jenna quirked a brow at him. "Apparently not hard enough," she said.

"Jenna's right," Clarissa agreed. "You're a police detective. It should be easy for you to figure out what's going on here."

But it wasn't, Grady thought, discomfited. "What I want to know right now is which one of you left this baby on Alec Roman's doorstep with this note."

Jenna accidentally nudged his arm with hers as she looked over his shoulder at the slightly worse-for-wear typewritten note he held in his hand. "To Andy's father, own up to your mistakes," Jenna read in a baffled voice.

Grady looked at his ex-wife. "Did you do it?" As much as he hated to admit it, even to himself, he could see Clarissa abandoning his child. After all, she had never wanted kids. Her promise to consider having them the last night they were together had been a last-ditch effort to save their failed marriage. Was it possible she had stopped taking the pill before she faked her domestic emergency and tricked him into showing up to save her? Had she gotten pregnant on purpose, then not told him about her pregnancy as punishment because he no longer loved her? If he ever really had.

Clarissa drew a deep breath. "Of course this baby is mine!"

"Oh, stop lying," Jenna snapped, completely losing her patience. "You know as well as I do, Clarissa, that Andy is my baby."

"You left him on Alec's doorstep?" Grady asked Jenna. As hard as he tried, he couldn't see that happening. Jenna's whole adult life had been devoted to rescuing abandoned children. The fact that they were both really into public service and helping others was the reason they'd hit it off so well that night they'd met last spring at Alec's party. But it wasn't the reason they'd left the party early and ended up in his bed, making wild, passionate love. That had all been due to chemistry. Had it been up to him, he never would have ended it the next morning. But Jenna had made it clear she wasn't interested in flings. She wanted marriage. Children. And from bitter experience Grady had known then, as he did now, that cops and marriage didn't mix.

"Look, Grady, things were crazy two weeks ago," Jenna began nervously. She paused and raked her lower lip with the edge of her teeth. "The bottom line is Andy never should have been left at Alec's. He should be home with me. And that's where he's going."

Her tone ticked Grady off, big-time. He'd had a hell of a shock when Jack had called him from California. Since then, he'd taken an emergency leave, completely rearranged his life, gotten his hopes up that at last he was going to have the baby he'd always wanted, and for what? To be the victim of a practical joke that should have ended days ago.

Oblivious to his thoughts, Jenna tossed her rich, full mane of wavy strawberry blond hair out of her face and continued to stalk purposefully around Grady's Philadelphia apartment. Grady watched as she swiftly gathered up blankets, diapers and bottles of formula as if she really was preparing to take the baby home with her. Her dark green eyes averted from him, she stuffed everything she had gathered into the overflowing diaper bag with a determined steadiness of purpose Grady found even more annoying.

In contrast, Grady's ex-wife of almost a year, Clarissa Noland, seemed in no hurry at all to leave. He watched as she shrugged out of her long white mink coat and dropped it with studied insouciance on the sofa next to the portable crib.

Clarissa caught Grady's eyes, smiled at him sexily, then turned to the baby sleeping contentedly inside the crib. Her pretty, aristocratic features lit up into a soft, pleased smile. She reached down and stroked the baby's tiny hand wonderingly, looking for a moment like she had just won the million-dollar lottery. But that, too, had to be fake, Grady surmised quickly, because Clarissa had never had a maternal urge in her body. That was part of what had made their marriage break up.

So it was back to his original premise. This had to be a gag. Hell, Grady sighed, considering he'd had the bad sense to sleep with both women in a two-week period, he probably deserved it. It didn't matter that neither interlude had been planned. He should have had better sense than to sleep with Clarissa out of pity, or go off with Jenna when they were both still on the rebound from their all-too-recent divorces, even if the attraction he'd felt for Jenna had been the most powerful attraction he'd ever felt for a woman in his life.

Jenna brushed past Grady in a whiff of lavender-scented perfume. She stooped to pick up a rattle that had fallen on the floor, stalked to the kitchen sink and washed it off thoroughly.

Grady started toward Jenna. Clarissa moved to cut him off and at the same time block either of their paths to the crib. "Hold on just a minute. You can't just walk out of here with my baby."

Jenna quirked a strawberry blond brow at Clarissa and stared at her in stunned silence. She dried off the rattle, marched to the diaper bag and put it inside, along with a stuffed bear. "You know, Clarissa," Jenna drawled, "if I were you, I'd think twice about making some outrageous claim here that you'll regret later."

"What's outrageous about having a baby with my ex-husband?" Clarissa retorted, in the same highly miffed tone. "Particularly when we never should've gotten divorced?"

Jenna narrowed her eyes at Clarissa. Her eyes flashed with a quick burst of temper. "I'm warning you, you lying troublemaker—" Jenna said. She took a warning step toward the crib. Clarissa stubbornly held her ground.

Jenna set the diaper bag on the floor beside her, her actions slow and deliberate. Straightening, she planted her hands on her waist. "Okay, we'll play it your way and go back to square one. Since when is this not my baby?" Jenna asked Clarissa very, very softly.

Clarissa tossed her head and folded her arms in front of her. "Since... always, of course."

Jenna grabbed a fistful of Clarissa's cerulean blue silk jumpsuit and brought her up short. "Listen, you. The last two weeks have been sheer hell for me. I'm about at the end of my patience—"

"As well as your rope," Grady put in, enjoying the show immensely.

Jenna let go of Clarissa's jumpsuit and stomped closer, not stopping until she and Grady were nose to nose. "I've about had it with you, too!" she warned him. Angry color washed her cheeks.

"Oh, have you now?" Grady taunted right back.

"Yes!"

Grady caught Jenna's hand before she could deliver a stinging slap to his face.

Behind her, Clarissa gasped and said, "Now that is going too far! I think you ought to arrest her, Grady!"

Grady wanted to do a lot of things to Jenna now that she had come back into his life again. Arresting her was the least of them. He forced her hand down between them. The skin of her wrist felt like hot silk beneath his palm. "Okay, Jenna," he schooled easily. "Enough drama."

"I couldn't agree more." Jenna's pretty chin jutted stubbornly. "And if you'll just let go of me—"

"That depends," Grady interrupted, "on whether you try to hit me again."

"And that depends," Jenna retorted, her wrist trembling slightly in his grip, "on whether you let me walk out of here with my baby or not."

Grady tried not to think how soft and hot her skin felt against his palm. How accessible in a very sexual way. Or how much he wanted to kiss Jenna again, Clarissa or no Clarissa. "And if I don't?"

"Then *I* might call the police," Jenna threatened, trembling a little more.

Grady gauged the temper in Jenna's eyes and saw it was cooling, coming under control again. Reluctantly, he released his hold on her. "Who does the baby belong to?" he asked firmly.

"I already told you! Andy is my baby!" both women declared in unison, then glared at one another as if they wanted to punch each other out.

Grady sighed. "The note said it was my baby."

"No, it didn't." The two women again spoke in unison. Clarissa picked up the note and read aloud. "All this typewritten note says is, *To Andy's father, own up to your mistakes.* It doesn't say you're the father at all."

"Right," Grady agreed sarcastically, "which is why, according to the lore being handed me, Alec and Jack both claimed Baby Andy as their own, too." He shook his head. This situation was too crazy to be real. "I'll give credit where it's due. You all really had me going."

"For the last time, Grady Noland, this isn't a joke," Clarissa said stiffly.

"Yes," Jenna agreed, taking Clarissa's side unexpectedly. She moved to stand next to her, both of them blocking Grady's way to the crib. "Andy is very real."

"Besides, you called me, remember?" Clarissa reminded as she gave him a steamy look that indicated she would be all too happy to adjourn immediately with him to his bedroom. "Just like I knew you would. We belong together, Grady," she continued softly, her pale blue eyes lifting persuasively to his. "I knew it before today and I certainly know it now."

Jenna stepped around them. "I'm glad the two of you have each other," Jenna said dryly. "And now that you do, Andy and I will leave you two to your reconciliation."

"Wait a minute. There isn't going to be a reconciliation," Grady said firmly, wanting there to be no illusions on anyone's part about that. He moved to bar Jenna's way to the crib. "Clarissa and I are divorced and we're going to stay that way."

"Not if I have anything to say about it," Clarissa said with a sly smile. She kept her eyes on his as she glided toward him and tucked both her elegantly manicured hands around his forearm. "That baby deserves two parents, Grady."

"Oh, I don't know about that. I think he could manage fine with just me," Jenna muttered as she buttoned her coat and looped the stuffed diaper bag over her shoulder. "And since Andy happens to be my baby—" she palmed her chest authoritatively "—I have the final say."

Clarissa continued to hang on Grady's arm. "Don't listen to her, Grady. You know as well as I do that can't be true."

Ignoring them both, Jenna picked up the tiny infant. He woke instantly. Looking at Jenna, Andy blinked, then gurgled happily at the sight of her and beamed her a toothless smile.

"Oh, precious," Jenna whispered to Andy. She bent and pressed a sweetly tender kiss on his forehead and whispered, "I have missed you so much, sweetheart. You just don't know..."

Grady watched tears stream down Jenna's face. Again, he was taken aback, both by the ludicrousness of the situation and the emotional force of Jenna's response. It was crazy. He almost wanted Andy to be Jenna's baby. And his. Even though they'd just been together that once. Even though everything in him told him this was all a little too loony to be true. And too loony not to be true...

"You see? He even knows me," Jenna whispered triumphantly through her tears.

"This proves nothing," Clarissa said hotly, "except that you have a way with children and an incredible imagination!"

"You're the one with the imagination, Clarissa." Jenna turned to Grady and sent him a stormy, accusing look that filled him with regret. He never should have walked away from Jenna the way he had after only one incredibly wonderful, incredibly perfect night together. "How can you not know whose baby this is?" she demanded of him.

"I think the answer to that is obvious," Clarissa said smoothly as she sat down and crossed her legs elegantly at the knee. "Grady and I still have feelings for one another. And the truth of the matter is, Jenna darling," she finished gently, "we always will."

"Now hold on a minute there, Clarissa," Grady said impatiently. He had been through this with his ex-wife, not once but many times.

As usual, Clarissa ignored him. "Why else would you have slept with me that night last April, just before our divorce became final?" she continued optimistically.

"Perhaps because your house had just been burglarized and you were scared out of your mind," Grady said. *And because I was a fool. A fool who felt guilty as hell because my marriage had failed.*

Clarissa shook her head at him, silently discounting his theory. "You're a cop, Grady. You don't sleep with all the women you rescue." She paused dramatically, gave him another telling look—one he was sure was meant to warn Jenna off. "Or do you?" she finished sweetly.

Grady gave his ex-wife a sharp glare. His patience was wearing extremely thin.

"The question is," Clarissa continued, rummaging through her bags and bringing out a pack of cigarettes, "why did you sleep with her?" She pointed to Jenna.

"Yes, Grady, I'd like to hear the answer to that myself," Jenna said softly. Her expression was stormy. "Why *did* you sleep with me that night?"

"The same reason you slept with me," Grady retorted gruffly. *Because I wanted you more than I ever wanted anyone in my life.* "Because we both concluded that fleeting love affairs with no strings were better all the way around."

Only they hadn't turned out to be, Grady admitted to himself in irritation. One night with Jenna, and it had spoiled it for him with every woman since; he'd probably want her the rest of his life. But he'd also known he hadn't a chance in hell of ever making a real go of it with Jenna, or any other woman, not if he wanted to stay a cop. So when she'd walked out, he had done as she asked and not pursued her, even though he knew in his heart that he should have.

His gaze gentled as he regarded Jenna. "Why did you sleep with me that night?" he asked softly. "Was it because you were on the rebound from your divorce? Or was it something else?" Since she hadn't pulled any punches, he didn't feel required to, either.

Jenna continued to hold Andy tenderly in her arms, and for a second their glances meshed. Grady felt the familiar electricity leap and sizzle between them.

Realizing what was about to happen, Jenna dropped her gaze and shook her head. She backed away from him, looking as if she wasn't about to go into that, now or at any other time. "None of this matters," Jenna said firmly in a flat, weary voice. Avoiding looking into his eyes again, she said, "I'm taking my baby and going home."

"Wait a minute!" Clarissa said. Grady turned to his ex-wife. For a second, he'd been so caught up with Jenna, he'd forgotten Clarissa was even in the room with them. "There's no proof that baby is yours, Jenna," she continued.

Color rushed into Jenna's cheeks, highlighting the delicate womanly curves of her cheekbones in the oval frame of her face. "I showed up to claim him, didn't I? More to the point, Grady didn't even have to call me to tell me to come and get Andy, as he did you."

Which was another reason Grady still wondered whether this was a practical joke. It was all unfolding a little too neatly and unexpectedly.

Clarissa sent Grady a sharp look. "You're not seriously listening to all of this, are you?" she asked.

Grady rubbed his jaw. "At this point, I don't know what to think," he drawled. "What kind of proof do you have, Jenna? A birth certificate?"

"Of course I have a birth certificate," Jenna cried.

"Then let's see it," Grady demanded tautly.

"That's not possible," Jenna said.

"And why, pray tell, is that?" Grady asked.

"Because it's not here. It's back at my farmhouse in Hudson Falls, in upstate New York," Jenna explained.

Clarissa rolled her eyes. "Likely story," she muttered beneath her breath.

Jenna arched a strawberry blond brow. "I don't see *you* handing over any legal proof, Clarissa."

Clarissa smiled at Jenna sweetly. "That's because I didn't bring mine with me, either. But then I didn't know about you, Jenna. If I had..." She lifted her slender shoulders in an elegant shrug. "Suffice it to say, I will produce all the necessary records just as soon as I can get back to my family home in Long Island to get them."

Grady turned to Clarissa with a frown. He wasn't sure the depth of emotions simmering within the two women could *all* be feigned. Which led him to wonder how much of what was going on was a put-on and how much was the truth. If there was anything he had learned in the course of his police work over the years, it was that almost nothing was exactly the way it first seemed.

Fortunately, his experience as a detective had taught him how to dig to uncover the truth. "You had the baby on Long Island?" he asked Clarissa.

"Don't tell me you actually expected me to go through something this traumatic alone?" Clarissa said.

Grady had no intention of getting into an argument about that with her. Ignoring his ex-wife's accusatory question as well as Jenna's temper-laced glare, Grady said, "Assuming this is true, why didn't either of you call me, and let me know you were pregnant? Why did you just dump him on Alec's doorstep with that note?"

"Because Alec was home," Clarissa was quick to point out before Jenna could speak. "You never are, Grady. You're always out working on a case."

"Alec thought the baby was his!" Grady replied.

"Well, that's certainly not our fault!" Jenna said cantankerously.

"Yes, but leaving the baby on the doorstep was. Why did you do it, Jenna, assuming it was you?"

She looked away evasively. Her soft lips tightened mutinously. "It's a long story. I really don't feel like going into it now," she muttered.

"Don't feel like going into it or can't—because it never happened?" Clarissa challenged.

Jenna glared at Clarissa. Grady shrugged. "It's a good point," he said.

"How kind of you to say so," Jenna flared, giving him another withering glare.

"See?" Clarissa said victoriously. "She has no proof, Grady, none at all."

"I have the most valid proof of all," Jenna said, looking at the baby cuddled so peacefully in her arms. "Andy loves me. He wants to be with me."

"That's no proof," Clarissa disagreed with an unfriendly sneer. "He loves me, too. And I'll prove it to you."

"Fine," Jenna said, her expression determined. "Go ahead. Show us how well you've bonded to my son." Reluctantly, she handed Andy over.

Andy went into Clarissa's gentle arms with wide-eyed wonder. Clarissa cooed at him softly. As he had with Jenna, Andy beamed her a toothless smile and cooed right back at her.

Jenna swore and ran a hand through her strawberry blond hair. "It's been so long since I've been with him I almost forgot. Andy is extremely sociable. In fact, he never met anyone he didn't like."

"Of course you would say that now," Clarissa harumphed.

Jenna turned to Grady desperately. "Look, I'll prove it to you, Grady," Jenna said. "I'll have a DNA blood test."

"So will I," Clarissa quickly volunteered.

"I can't believe this," Grady muttered. "You're both going to stand there and continue to claim this baby?"

The corners of Jenna's mouth curved up in a grim parody of a smile. "Looks that way, doesn't it?" she said.

"OKAY, ALEC, YOU WIN," Grady said as soon as the long-distance operator had patched him through to Paris. "This is without a doubt the very best practical joke you and Jack ever played on me."

"What joke?" Alec said, sounding genuinely confused.

Grady sighed. He was getting very tired of spelling everything out. "The baby. Your marriage."

"Baby Andy is no joke, Grady. Jack and I are seriously looking for his parents," Alec answered. He paused. "Jack told me you were sure Andy was your son."

Alec sounded concerned, Grady realized uncomfortably, then pushed the thought aside. "I also told him there were two candidates for his mother."

"Neither claimed Andy?" Alec guessed.

"Both claimed him," Grady said.

Alec started to laugh. "You're kidding, right?"

"Don't pretend you don't know anything about this," Grady advised shortly.

"I only wish," Alec said wistfully.

Grady paused. Neither Alec nor Jack had ever been shy about claiming victory, he realized uneasily. Hence, Alec's confusion could only mean one thing. He muttered an oath. "You swear on the sacredness of our friendship this is no joke?" Grady demanded.

"I swear," Alec said firmly. "My marriage to Jade is real enough, though. Jade, say hi to Grady."

A soft, melodious voice came on the phone. "Hi, Grady."

"Hi, Jade," Grady said.

"Believe me now?" Alec asked as he got back on the line.

"Yeah, sure," Grady said. So that was one down. "Jack—"

"Is not in on it, either, Grady," Alec said.

"How do you know?" Grady demanded.

"Because both Jack and I already went through what you're going through now," Alec said calmly. "Listen to me, Grady. This is no joke. If it were, I would have owned up to it right away. You know that."

Yeah, Grady did, that was what was so troubling. Another silence fell. Aware both women were watching him and hanging on his every word, Grady ran his hand through his hair and swore softly.

"Sounds like you got yourself in a heap of trouble there, pal," Alec said. "So. What are you going to do?"

Grady turned to see both Jenna and Clarissa glaring at him. Only Andy was smiling and gurgling happily, maybe because he intuited that three people were fighting to take care of him. "The only thing I can do," Grady said grimly, as the realization of just how big a mess he was really in sank in. "I'm going to the hospital and taking those blood tests."

"HOW LONG before we get the results?" Jenna asked the lab tech at Philadelphia General Hospital impatiently. She couldn't believe Clarissa was still continuing the charade. She'd thought the other woman would give up before the blood tests were taken. But no, Clarissa had brazened her way through the tests just as if she really had delivered Andy herself. Part of Jenna could almost understand why. Clarissa was still deeply in love with Grady, even though Grady didn't appear to be in love with Clarissa now. If he ever had been, she thought. Somehow, she just couldn't see the two of them together. They were all wrong for one another.

"I'll put a rush on it, but it'll be a few days, at the very least," the lab tech said. He was young, efficient and, to Jenna's dismay, completely gaga over the elegant Clarissa.

"Great," Grady muttered, looking more impatient than ever to know what was really going on.

"In the meantime, I'll keep Andy," Jenna said quickly.

"No, in the meantime, I'm keeping Andy," Grady corrected.

"How?" Jenna shot back. "You have to work, remember?"

"Easy." Grady's intent gray-blue gaze meshed with hers. For a second, Jenna wished she wasn't so attracted to him. But the simple truth of the matter was there wasn't an inch of Grady Noland's tall, broad-shouldered frame she didn't find altogether too attractive. She liked the way he dressed—in jeans, oxford cloth shirts—today's was light blue—Harris tweed jackets—today's was gray—and boots. There was nothing soft or easy about him, and yet he was capable of great tenderness, especially in bed. "I've already called the station and arranged for an emergency leave."

Jenna looked into his intent gray-blue gaze. "You can't seriously expect me to let you keep my baby?" she said, and saw the hollows beneath his cheekbones grow more pronounced.

Grady shrugged indifferently. "The way I see it, this baby was abandoned to my care, if not directly, then indirectly, so yes, Jenna, that is exactly what I expect." His eyes probed hers relentlessly, searching for any signs of playfulness or duplicity. "Unless you can produce proof that he's yours between now and then?"

"No problem," Clarissa was quick to put in. "In fact, I'm going home to Long Island to get my proof right now."

"Fake birth certificates can be made up anywhere," Jenna said. She was beginning to feel really uneasy about all of this. Particularly since she knew her own "proof" wouldn't stand up to anyone's scrutiny, never mind the scrutiny of a crack Philadelphia police detective.

"Honestly, Jenna, you are so suspicious," Clarissa said. She turned to Grady as proprietorially as if she still was his wife. "My proof won't be fake," Clarissa reassured her ex-husband bluntly, with a great deal more confidence than Jenna felt.

"Mine isn't, either," Jenna promised. Though how the hell she was going to deliver on that promise, she didn't know. She really should have thought this all out beforehand. But then, hindsight was always better, particularly in complicated situations like this, she reassured herself.

"I'll be the judge of the proof," Grady said, giving both of them a hard look. "In the meantime, Andy and I bid you two adieu."

"I KNOW what you're thinking, kid, you're thinking this is all my fault," Grady said to Andy as he drove them both to his apartment. "That I'm just getting a dose of my own medicine. And you're right. I never should have slept with Clarissa that night, even if her apartment had been broken into. But she was so damn needy and vulnerable, and I hadn't been with anyone in so long... Okay, so that's still no excuse. Or even an explanation. But I'm not sure how I can explain how I felt at that time. Lonely. Sad that my marriage to Clarissa was over. And guilty as hell, because I felt I'd let her down. She needed me that night, and I thought my being there for her might somehow make up for my not loving her, only I was wrong. Dead wrong. It only made things worse. When her apartment was burglarized again, I sent someone else to check it out. Shortly after that, she moved back to Long Island to be with her parents. And that was that, or so I thought," Grady finished with a sigh.

Andy gurgled and waved his rattle. Grady grinned at him. He was glad the little guy, with his cherubic face, bright blue eyes and fuzzy dark brown hair, was such a trooper. "Okay. Enough about Clarissa. You want to know how I got involved with Jenna, don't you? Well, it was like this. I met her at a party at Alec's. You know Alec, don't you? Anyway, it was one of those stiff formal business parties where everyone drinks very little and eats even less and talks business the whole night long and I was not in the mood to mingle.

"So I was trying to sneak out the back way and I found Jenna also trying to sneak out the back way. Damn, she was beautiful. We got to laughing about how dull Alec's party was and we took a bottle of his champagne and we walked to my place and talked about how fed up we both were with marriage, the institution, and what a good thing it would be just to sleep with someone because you felt like it, and not worry about tomorrow, or the consequences of your actions, and the next thing I knew we were in my bed...." Grady sighed again. "When I woke up the next morning, she was already gone. She left me a note—seems that woman is big on notes—saying that it had been fun, but she wasn't looking for a relationship. She asked me not to call her or try to see her." Grady parked in front of his apartment and got out, Andy in his arms.

"That was a hard one," Grady continued conversationally as Andy gazed up at him attentively. "I wanted to see Jenna again. Boy, did I ever want to see her again. But I also knew I was all wrong for her,'' Grady said as he walked up the steps and paused to check the mail. ''Even though Jenna said she had concluded she wasn't the marrying kind, her eyes, those beautiful dark green eyes of hers, said nothing but marriage was ever really going to do for a woman like her. And I had already proved that cops and marriage don't mix.''

Grady stuffed his mail into his pocket, then shut the mailbox. ''She couldn't be telling the truth, could she? She couldn't really be your mother?'' Grady asked and looked at Andy briefly before he unlocked the door to his apartment. Withdrawing the key from the lock, he shifted Andy in his arms. ''I mean, none of this makes sense to me. I can see Jenna having you by herself because that's just the type of gutsy woman she is—but I can't see her leaving you on Alec's doorstep, even if it was Valentine's Day,'' Grady continued as he went inside.

''You're right,'' Jenna said softly, stepping from the shadows of his apartment. Her eyes were smudged with tears, and more desperate than he could ever have imagined them being. ''I wouldn't have done that, Grady. I would never have left Andy alone like that, even for a second.''

Grady took a moment to register the fact that Jenna was in his apartment, uninvited this time. He didn't want to think about how fast she'd had to drive her rental car to get here ahead of him, or how much she'd had to bribe the superintendent to get into his apartment. "Then how do you explain it?" he asked, part of his heart hardening at the duplicity she'd had to employ to get her way.

"Simple," Jenna said. She looked at Grady beseechingly and took a deep, bolstering breath. "Andy was kidnapped."

Chapter Two

"What do you mean Andy was kidnapped?" Grady said.

"Exactly what I said. He was taken from his crib while he was sleeping."

Grady took Andy out of his snowsuit and placed him in the crib. He gave the mobile music box a few swift turns. Andy gurgled as the Disney characters began spinning round above him.

Satisfied the baby was content for the moment, Grady turned to Jenna. She had taken her coat off this time. She looked pale. Stressed out. And scared. Like a kidnapping really had occurred. But that was impossible, wasn't it? "Where were you when this happened?" Grady bit out impatiently.

Jenna wrung her hands in front of her nervously. "In the office on the first floor of my family's upstate New York farmhouse." Her voice was quiet, subdued.

"And Andy was—"

"Upstairs, in the nursery."

His thoughts spinning, Grady walked into the kitchen. He grabbed a cold Coke Classic from the refrigerator and popped the top open. He offered one to her. She shook her head. Grady took a long sip and lounged against the counter. "Let me get this straight. Someone just came into the house—"

Jenna's chin tipped defiantly. Some of the color came back into her cheeks. "Yes!"

Grady quirked a brow in quiet disbelief, but kept his voice neutral. "And you didn't hear anything," he surmised.

"No."

The seconds strung out tensely. "How is that possible?" Jenna shrugged and looked away. *She's holding something back.* "Were your doors unlocked?" Grady persisted.

Jenna stalked back and forth, scowling at him. "No. Of course not."

Grady took another long swallow of Coke. "Then how did this kidnapper get in?"

"I don't know." Jenna shrugged and spread her hands in front of her helplessly. "I suppose he had a key."

"Which he got where?" Grady asked.

Jenna's straight white teeth raked across her unglossed lower lip. Grady could tell from the way she hesitated that she was considering not answering that. He continued staring at her, waiting. She bit her lip again, looked away and said finally, "Maybe from the fake rock in the flower garden, among the real rocks."

"Are you guessing that or do you know for sure?"

Jenna clamped her arms in front of her like a shield. "I know for sure."

Grady took another long drink. "And this happened when?"

"Midmorning, Valentine's Day."

Grady paused, working hard to marshal his emotions. "Did you call the police?"

Again, Jenna shook her head. "No."

"Why not?"

She lounged against the opposite counter and regarded him wearily. "Do we have to get into this?"

He inclined his head. "Only if you want me to believe your story."

She was silent, thinking. Finally she dragged a hand through her hair and admitted in a low, troubled voice, "I didn't call the police because I knew it was an inside job, probably by some well-meaning member of my family."

Grady put his can aside, aware—even if Jenna wasn't—that this was suddenly getting very serious. "How did you know that?" he asked brusquely.

Jenna's full lips tightened. She lifted her glance and regarded him with obvious resentment. "A couple of things. When I moved out to the farmhouse last summer, I had a security system installed. It was that morning Nanny Beth—that's Andy's governess—left the house to go into town on errands."

"And you confirmed this with Nanny Beth?"

"Actually—" Jenna paused again "—I haven't been able to talk to her since the kidnapping."

Grady's pulse picked up. He had the feeling this was about to get a lot more complicated. "Why not?" he asked mildly.

Jenna treated him to a careless smile. "I don't know where she is."

Grady paused. So much of what she'd already told him simply didn't add up. She said she'd recently had a baby. Yet she was reed thin, and judging from the fit of those tight jeans and long white sweater, in fine physical shape. She said her baby had been kidnapped over two weeks ago, yet she hadn't called the police, hadn't even come to see him until now, and she said he was the father! More, she had known all along that he was a cop and could have helped her locate the baby. More incriminating still, she seemed to think she was in the right here. And that didn't add up, either. "You're telling me you think your nanny is the kidnapper?" Grady asked calmly.

"Of course not! Nanny's been with my family for years."

"Where is she now?"

"I don't know."

"Did you fire her?"

"No."

"Did she quit?"

"No, but—" Jenna hesitated. "She may have taken a few days off."

"Wouldn't she have told you if she was going to do that?"

"Normally, yes—"

"But?"

Jenna shrugged. "But she didn't this time, that's all."

"I'm going to have to put out an APB on her."

Jenna grabbed his arm. "No, Grady, don't." He looked at her. "Can't you just look for Nanny unofficially?" Jenna pleaded softly. "I'm sure she didn't do anything criminal."

"And how do you know that?" Grady drawled.

Jenna's chin took on a stubborn tilt. "Because I know her. She loves me and she loves Andy very much. She would never do anything to hurt us."

Grady paused. "I'm going to have to talk to Nanny anyway before this is all over," he warned.

"All right." Jenna sighed. "I'll help you find her. But in the meantime, we've got to try to figure out who kidnapped Andy from the farmhouse." Her dark green eyes looked directly into his. "Whoever broke into the farmhouse knew the code to turn off the security system. They used it to get into the house without setting off the alarm."

Grady picked up his can of Coke and drained it. "Who else knows the code?" He set the can on the counter with a thud.

"My father, my brother and his wife, and Nanny."

He folded his arms in front of him. "Why would they want to kidnap Andy?"

Jenna shrugged and looked evasive again. "Because they thought they were doing me a favor by getting Andy's father involved?"

Grady decided he'd played good cop long enough. It was time to crowd her and put on the pressure. He pushed away from the counter and, arms still folded in front of him, towered over her. "How do you figure that?"

Jenna swallowed hard and rummaged in her purse. "By this note that was left."

Grady unfolded the paper. He had to step back a pace to study it. Like the note left with Andy when he arrived at Alec's, this was typewritten in capital letters. It read, "Every baby needs a father, Jenna. The responsibility for Andy is not yours alone." There was a postscript. "Don't worry and don't call the police. Andy'll be well taken care of until he is reunited with his father."

Grady folded the note. "Mind if I keep this?"

Jenna glared at him. "That all depends on what you're going to do with it."

He slipped the note into his pocket. "Am I making you nervous, Jenna?"

"The fact that you're a cop is making me nervous."

"Why? You say you didn't do anything wrong."

"I didn't," she said quickly.

"Then—"

"Look." Jenna released a frustrated breath. Her fingertips trembled as she rearranged her strawberry blond hair. "I've explained the situation to you. Regardless of what that note says, Andy is not your responsibility."

Grady smiled mirthlessly. "There we differ, babe."

"Excuse me?"

"If Andy's my child, then he damn well is my responsibility."

"Fine, then he's not your child."

"It's a little too late to be saying that, don't you think?"

Jenna released another frustrated breath. The color in her cheeks turned from a pale pink to a dusky rose. "All I want to do is take my baby and go home, Grady." She spoke as if underlining every word.

"Not until we have proof that he is your baby," Grady stipulated softly, "and maybe not even then."

It was Jenna's turn to stomp closer. "Why the hell not?"

Grady held his ground, despite the fact they were now uncomfortably close. Close enough for him to smell the flowery fragrance of her hair and skin. Close enough for him to see the luminous depths of her dark green eyes, and the kissable softness of her lips and skin. His mood grim, Grady stared down at her. "Because there's still a lot I don't understand," he said gruffly.

Jenna's lower lip thrust toward him contentiously. "Such as?"

Grady's lower body was thrumming. He braced his legs a little farther apart and fought his attraction to her. "Such as why you let a whole two weeks go by before you came to see me today," he said softly.

Jenna turned away and moved to the end of the counter. "I told you." She gripped the edge of the counter tightly with one hand. "I thought someone in the family had him, and I was looking for him myself."

She's hiding something, Grady thought. "But if you knew the kidnapper planned to take Andy to me and I'm Andy's father—"

"The kidnapper didn't know you were his father!" she interrupted emotionally, pivoting to him once more. "No one did. I had 'unknown' put on the birth certificate."

Grady blinked. "You did what?"

"You heard me."

"Heard you, yes," Grady replied between gritted teeth. "Understand you, no."

Jenna smiled. Her look was deliberately provoking. "Exactly why I didn't call you," she said sweetly.

"You could have let me know you were pregnant," Grady accused tightly. His muscles were rigid with suppressed anger and resentment. Hurt.

"Why?" Jenna shot back without missing a beat. Her eyes glittered hotly as she reminded him softly, "You made it very clear to me that night we were together that since your divorce, you were no longer the marrying kind."

"As I recall at the time, neither were you."

"Right," Jenna said flatly. She moved away from him with an insouciant shrug. "Andy didn't change that."

"*Au contraire,* babe." Grady stepped around her quickly and blocked her exit from the galley kitchen. "Andy here changes everything. If he's your child."

"What's that supposed to mean?"

"It means I'm still not convinced you're telling me the truth." She hadn't presented nearly enough facts to substantiate her story. In his years as a police detective, Grady had learned to trust only the facts, not people's heartrending stories or one-sided views, or even his own emotions, which in this case were jumping up and down with joy at the thought of having a child of his own at long last.

"If you didn't tell anyone who Andy's father was, then how could they figure out who to take Andy to?"

"I presume by going through my files, checking out my social calendar and putting two and two together." Jenna swallowed hard. "The night Andy was conceived, I was in Philadelphia for Alec's party. Alec's address and phone number were written down as the emergency contact number I left with my office. Obviously, someone put two and two together and figured Alec Roman was the father because that's where I'd been exactly nine months before Andy was born. Only I wasn't with Alec that night, I was with you."

"How well do you know Alec?"

Jenna shrugged. "I met him several years ago at a charity fund-raiser for the Children's Hospital. He was interested in my work with the Children's Rescue Foundation and has even loaned me the use of his jet a couple times for foundation business."

"So it's possible someone would think you to be—"

"More than friends, yes. We're not."

"What kind of proof did you bring with you to substantiate this theory?" Grady asked.

Again, she paled. "Proof?" Jenna gulped and stepped away from him uneasily.

"Yeah, proof," Grady repeated impatiently.

"I showed up here today to get Andy."

"A good two weeks after the alleged kidnapping," Grady agreed. Silence fell between them. It was thick with tension. And Jenna was a million miles away from him, in her thoughts. Grady didn't recall Jenna behaving so mysteriously last spring. "Why didn't you call me sooner if you had figured all this out?" he persisted.

Jenna glared at him. "I tried to get in touch with you earlier."

"When?"

"On Valentine's Day. I called you at the station shortly after I realized Andy was missing. I was pretty hysterical at the time. I told your buddies there that it was an emergency."

Grady frowned at the simmering resentment in her eyes. "And—?"

Jenna paced to the refrigerator, to the stove, the dishwasher, and then back again. "And they laughed at me." She yanked open the refrigerator door, pulled out the Coke Classic he had offered her earlier and popped the tab. "They said that everyone was having 'romantic emergencies' that day, but you were out on a case and *my* 'romantic emergency' with you would just have to wait."

Her words had a disturbing ring of truth. "I never got your message."

Jenna glared at him. Her eyes were an icy green. "Never got it or just decided not to return my call?"

"Never got it!" Grady said.

She shook her head and took a long draft of Coke. "And you expect me to believe that?"

"If I believe you, yeah, I do," Grady shot back. "Besides, your call should be easy enough to trace. All calls to the station are logged in by computer."

Jenna lifted her gaze and inclined her head slightly to one side. "Meaning what? My word alone isn't good enough?"

"Your story has more holes than a sieve."

She wanted to retreat. Deciding against that option, she shifted away from him and took another long, thirsty drink. "I want my baby back."

"You're going to have to prove he's your baby first." *And then,* Grady amended silently, *you're going to have to prove to me you didn't abandon him.*

"I'm not leaving here without him."

Grady looked at her mouth, which was damp and soft. He wanted to drag her into his arms and kiss her again, reason be damned. He wanted to take her to his bed and make wild passionate love to her again, and then, only then, when they'd exhausted themselves, run the gamut of their feelings for one another, only then deal with this mess. But that was impossible.

He still had Clarissa to deal with. And Andy...

"Or, if you'd rather, I'll stay here with you and I'll help you take care of Andy until we get the results of the blood tests back," Jenna offered.

"No," Grady said.

Abruptly, she looked exhausted and close to tears. "Grady, please," she whispered. "Don't do this to me. Don't take my baby from me."

Regardless of what Jenna might think about him, he did not want to see her get down on her knees and beg. Nor did he want to forcibly part her from her child—if Andy was hers. He tugged a hand through his dark brown hair. "Look, Jenna," he began wearily, "it's been an incredibly long day—"

Jenna blinked rapidly and recovered her composure. In a voice thick with emotion, she predicted, "Knowing Andy, it's going to be even longer." Their glances meshed, and Jenna continued informatively, "He doesn't sleep through the night yet, remember? And there's something else."

Grady regarded her warily, his heart working like a trip-hammer in his chest. "What?"

Jenna released a worried sigh. Her eyes lifted to his. "We can't forget Andy was kidnapped once. I still don't know who did it."

Grady searched her face. For months, he had told himself memory had exaggerated her stunning good looks, the creamy complexion, perfect smile and long-lashed green eyes. Not so. She was even better now. Her cheekbones were more pronounced, her voice throatier, her mouth softer, more tempting. So tempting, in fact, he was having trouble concentrating on the business at hand.

"Assuming I'm able to solve this mystery for you, Jenna, do you want this kidnapper prosecuted?" he asked. He was curious to see what her reaction would be. If she was making it all up, the answer would of course be no. On the other hand, she could easily be out for vengeance, her target anyone from her ex-husband to a neighbor she didn't like. In his years as a cop, he'd seen it all.

Jenna drew in a wavering breath. "I want to make sure it doesn't happen again. To that end," she said slowly, "a promise and a confession from the meddlesome abductor will do."

"I see," Grady said slowly. "And what if that's not good enough for me, Jenna? As the baby's father, I certainly should have some say."

She drew in a second unsteady breath. "You don't want any trouble here, either, Grady." And suddenly he knew she was holding back at least as much as she had already told him. He'd never had much patience with people who told less than the truth, either before or after he became a cop.

"What makes you so sure of that?" Grady asked silkily as, without warning, the anger that had been building in him all afternoon took off like a rocket hurtling into space.

Dammit, if Andy was his baby and Jenna's, as she had just claimed, Jenna had robbed him not only of the chance to marry her and save their child from being born illegitimately, but she had also deprived him of his own baby's birth and the first eight weeks of his son's life. Hell, he might have gone to his grave never knowing he had a child. His son would have been similarly uninformed, senselessly hurt and denied a dad. And for what? So Jenna wouldn't have to sacrifice her pride?

"Maybe I like trouble," he speculated brashly. And maybe it was time she learned that she couldn't shut him out that way, not out of his own child's life and maybe not out of hers, either. Not if he wanted in. And right now, as it happened, he did. If he had a child, he was damn well going to be around to raise it. Even if it meant sharing that baby, as well as the whole parenting process, with her.

He stepped toward her, his decision made. She stepped back.

"Grady, don't," she said shakily.

"Don't what?" Grady asked. They continued their silent two-step until her back was against the wall. Grady was directly in front of her. She attempted to move past him, but this time he wasn't about to let her go, not until he had the whole truth and nothing but the truth from her. He put a hand out to block her escape and stared down at her grimly. "The way I look at it, if everything you've just now told me is true, you owe me big time for this, Jenna."

Hot, angry color flared in her cheeks. "Everything I've told you is true!" she shot back emotionally as Grady braced a hand flat against the wall on either side of her. "But that doesn't mean I owe you anything," Jenna continued.

Grady uttered a mirthless laugh. Their bodies weren't quite touching, but he could see her trembling. He could recall with stunning clarity the soft give of her slender body. He quirked a brow. "Oh, no?"

"No."

"Meaning what? That you never would have told me we had a child together had Andy not been kidnapped? That you would have let me go to my grave never knowing I had a son?"

Jenna swallowed and stared up at him. She didn't know what she had expected, coming back to see Grady this way. She had only known she couldn't leave Philadelphia without her baby. And she couldn't gain custody of Andy with Clarissa around, foolishly muddying the situation and insisting on *her* rights. So she'd doubled back to Grady's apartment after the DNA tests, figuring that a little one-on-one conversation with him would give her the opportunity to explain as little as was humanly possible about what had transpired in the last two weeks in order to get her back her baby.

She had known, of course, that it wouldn't be easy. Grady was stubborn and opinionated to a fault, just as she was. Furthermore, he had every right to be angry and resentful because she hadn't told him about the baby. He thought it was because she'd been selfish and hadn't wanted to share their child, but she knew in her heart just the opposite was true. She'd been trying to protect her child, and herself, from rejection the best way she knew how. She hadn't wanted to force Grady into fatherhood, even from a distance. Particularly when she knew full well how he felt about marriage. Her breasts rose and lowered with every quick, shaky breath she drew. "I don't see where my telling you or not telling you enters into this," Jenna retorted stubbornly.

"Answer the question, Jenna!"

"All right!" Her palms flattened against his chest, holding him at bay. "I had decided not to tell you."

Grady tried not to think about how it felt to have her touching him again. He tried not to recall what a sensual, giving lover she had been and instead concentrated on his hurt at having been shut out of the most important experience of his life. "Why?"

"Because," Jenna explained. She tilted her head against the wall and her voice rose emotionally as she spoke. "It wasn't necessary for me to drag you into this, not when Andy already had me, and a home, and enough money to buy him everything he ever needed or wanted."

Grady's exasperation mounted until he felt as though he was going to explode. He studied her silently. "He still didn't have a father, Jenna."

To Grady's consternation, Jenna refused to admit she'd done anything wrong. "We could have worked around that," she insisted stubbornly.

"Oh, yeah?" Grady said grimly, as his frustration mounted. "Well, let's see how well you work around this, Jenna." Beyond all thought except the desire to bring her back to some semblance of reality, he tunneled his hands through her hair and lifted her face to his. Ignoring her soft, muted gasp of dismay, he lowered his mouth to hers and then did what he had been wanting to do since the first moment he'd laid eyes on her again.

He kissed her like they'd never been apart. He kissed her to remind her what they had shared, and what they could share again, given half a chance. He kissed her because he had missed her. Because they'd let so many things drive them apart.

She fought him at first, using her hands to push against his chest. He persisted, parting her lips with the pressure of his, nudging his tongue inside, tasting the sweetness that was her, tormenting her with lazy sweeps of his tongue again and again until she trembled. He deepened the kiss pleasurably, and Jenna moaned. Her whole body softened. The pressure of her hands on his chest turned from a show of resistance to a bittersweet caress.

Satisfaction rushed through Grady as he felt her knees give out, just a little. The next thing he knew her arms were wrapped around his neck, pulling him close, and she was kissing him back with utter abandon.

His thoughts spinning, Grady struggled to keep the upper hand in their ongoing battle of wills. Kissing her was just a way to make a point, he told himself sternly. To let her see firsthand what it felt like to have an intimate part of her life decided without her prior knowledge or consent. He couldn't let this embrace get out of hand.

But before he knew it the tide had changed again. Her body molded to his, and her kiss turned even sweeter, more seductively compelling. Waves of desire arced through him. Hungry for more of her, needing more of her, needing more of this, he pressed even closer. He knew the risk in his action, even as his heart pounded and the blood rushed into his groin.

Making love to Jenna was about as safe as stepping out onto a ledge of a high rise without a safety rope, but then, Grady thought as he uttered a contented sigh and dove even deeper into the passionate embrace, he had always liked living on the edge....

He wrapped an arm around her and pulled her closer yet.

Without warning, Jenna broke off the kiss and pushed him away. "You shouldn't have done that," she said, trembling.

Grady saw her response and grinned in male satisfaction. "You're right, I shouldn't have," he said without apology, then quirked a thoughtful brow at her. "But now that I have...now that you know nothing about our attraction to each other has changed, maybe now you'll understand why you should leave."

Jenna lifted her eyes heavenward. Abruptly, she was her old sassy self. "Look, Grady, if you think one little kiss—"

"One long, steamy kiss," he corrected.

Jenna ignored him and plowed on determinedly. "Is going to have me darting out of here like a scared child, you have another think coming."

He regarded her with a look of utter male supremacy. "Is that so?" he drawled.

"That is definitely so," Jenna said. She might not have made love with anyone at all except Grady outside of marriage, but that didn't mean she couldn't be adult about it. So they'd succumbed to temptation and slept together a year ago. It had happened, but it was over. Both were smarter now. And she, at least, had learned her lesson and was a hell of a lot more restrained, as she had just proved to herself by breaking off their fiery kiss, instead of allowing it to lead her into his bed. Courageously holding Grady's gaze, Jenna continued flatly, "Because I'm still not going anywhere without Andy."

Grady sighed and stepped back. "Come on, Jenna," he said, suddenly making no effort to hide his complete exasperation with her, "I don't want to have to get ugly here and throw you out."

The truth be told, Jenna didn't want that, either. She took a deep breath and called upon all the powers of feminine persuasion she possessed. She had already proved to herself that she couldn't get to Grady, person to person. She might, however, be able to get to him woman to man. It was a risk, of course, but one she was willing to take. "If you do what I want," she promised throatily, "you won't have to."

Grady stared at her in complete fascination, stunned into silence by her abrupt change of mood. His eyes took a slow, studied tour of her body, then returned with sensual deliberation to her face. "If this is the kind of proposal I think it is, you'd better spell it out, babe."

"If we leave now, and drive all evening, we can be at my farmhouse by midnight," Jenna proposed with as much serenity as she could muster.

Grady's steely blue glance narrowed suspiciously. He folded his arms and leaned against the counter. "Why would we want to do that?"

Jenna held his gaze with effort. She fixed him with the sort of smile she usually saved for recalcitrant contributors to her foundation, the Children's Rescue Foundation. "You said you wanted proof Andy is mine," she reminded pleasantly.

"That's right," Grady replied amiably as his expression hardened implacably. "I do."

"Well—" Jenna shrugged "—the proof is there." *And Clarissa is not.*

Grady shifted and stood even straighter. His steely blue gaze grew even more probing. "What kind of proof?"

"His birth certificate and baby footprints, for one thing. The nursery where he's slept since he was born. The pictures of him as a newborn. Even the clothes he's already outgrown. Please, Grady. Just come with me," she urged.

Once he was there, he would see what a good mother she was. He would know it was okay to leave the baby in her very capable care. He would know she had done what was best for all three of them from the very first, and that was not to force them into any domestic arrangement that was destined to make them all miserable, just because they'd been blessed with an unexpected surprise.

"We can turn my rental car in on the way out of town and then drive up to Hudson Falls," Jenna continued persuasively.

"In my car."

"Yes. It won't be quite as fast as flying but it'll be easier in the sense that we'll be traveling with a baby and able to stop whenever or wherever we need to."

"This better not be a wild-goose chase," Grady growled.

Jenna's spirits soared as she realized Grady was finally of a mind to cooperate with her. "It won't be," she promised.

Chapter Three

"How much farther?" Grady asked wearily several hours later.

"About fifteen miles."

He glanced at the rolling countryside on either side of the two-lane country road. Trees were plentiful. Farmhouses were few and far between. "You really are out in the country," he said. A city guy himself, he had never understood the allure of living out in the sticks.

Jenna smiled and settled back in her seat. She hadn't put Andy down since she'd given him his bottle. And though he had long since fallen back to sleep, seeing how utterly contented Jenna looked, just holding the sleeping baby in her arms, Grady didn't have the heart to suggest she put him in his car seat, even if it would be a more comfortable way for her to travel.

"I know." Jenna sighed as she dipped her head and pressed a tender kiss on the top of Andy's head. She laid her cheek against his soft, dark hair and breathed in his baby scent. "That's one of the things I like best about the area. The complete absence of city noise and traffic."

"Why did you move all the way out here?"

Jenna shrugged and tucked Andy's blanket around his sleeper-covered feet. "Baxter and I put our house in Albany on the market at the time we divorced. When it finally sold last June, I needed a place to live."

"Surely you could have bought another house in Albany."

"I could have. But with my family's Hudson Falls farmhouse standing empty and me needing a break from public life anyway, it made sense for me to go there. Particularly since I was pregnant and unmarried." She gave him a steady look and pointed out the next turn. "I did not want to bear the brunt of a scandal."

Grady shrugged. Even if Jenna hadn't wanted to marry him, and he admitted he hadn't been a very marriageable guy a year ago, he and Jenna still could've been together. "These days—"

Jenna shook her head and shifted Andy closer to her breast. "It doesn't matter to my father what anyone else does. He cares about me. Unwed pregnancies are not de rigueur in my family."

In Grady's, either, he realized uncomfortably. "You could have asked me to marry you," he pointed out evenly. In fact, part of him wished she had.

Jenna smirked and pointed out yet another turn. "With or without a shotgun?" she asked wryly.

He ignored her as he turned onto a country road that was barely wide enough for his car. "I would have done the honorable thing."

"That's just it, Grady. I didn't want you to do the honorable thing. Besides," she continued confidently, "I had it all worked out."

Grady's hand tightened on the steering wheel. Irritation colored his low voice. "Worked out, how?"

"I was going to tell everyone Andy was adopted. They know I see a lot of orphaned children in the course of my work for the foundation. Everyone knows how softhearted I am. I don't think it would surprise anyone to see me adopt one of the children the Rescue Foundation has aided."

Grady swore silently at her naïveté. "What about me?"

"You'd be off the hook."

Grady exhaled slowly. "Don't you think that's a decision I should have made?" He glanced at her in the dim light of the dash. Jenna's mouth tightened.

"Maybe I would have let you make it had you ever called again."

Touché, Grady thought. She pointed out another turn, this one at a mailbox at the end of a long country lane. "You know why I didn't," Grady said as he guided the car onto the driveway that led to a plain white farmhouse a good half mile back from the road. "We agreed before we ever went to my place that night that it was only going to be a one-night thing."

"It didn't turn out that way for me." Jenna glanced out the window.

"Yes, but I didn't know that."

"It doesn't matter," she said and held the baby closer.

There she was very wrong. "It does to me," Grady said. He parked in front of the farmhouse and cut the ignition. He turned to her, no longer sure if this was a bad dream or a lifelong fantasy come true. He only knew for certain that if this was his baby, he wanted Andy's mother to be Jenna. And if it wasn't their child, then...then he still wanted Jenna. He wanted to make love to her at least one more time.

Kissing her had stirred something deep inside him, something he had thought was dead. And though he wasn't sure that such wild passion was good for anything except getting him into trouble, he still wanted to experience it again. Hell, after five hours of being confined in a car with Jenna, smelling her perfume and listening to her soft throaty voice, he wanted to kiss her again, and would have if she hadn't been holding the baby like a shield in front of her.

Jenna studied his face a moment longer, then sighed wearily. "Let's just go inside. I'll put Andy down in the nursery, and then I'll show you the birth certificate and so forth."

Grady shrugged and warned himself not to get his hopes up. "The hospital ID bracelet would also be nice," Grady said. He got out of the car and rushed around to help her.

Jenna carried Andy up the walk while he followed with the diaper bag, her purse and several suitcases. "Um, I wasn't in a hospital, exactly."

He leaned against the portal as she punched in a security code that would shut off the silent alarm and then another that would unlock the door. "Where did you have the baby?"

Jenna waited until the panel blinked okay, then pushed open the door. "Here," she said.

"You're kidding, right?"

Jenna gave him a placating smile, which only annoyed Grady. "There wasn't time to get to the hospital," Jenna said calmly.

Shifting Andy higher in her arms, Jenna stepped across the threshold. Grady followed. The house was cozy, warm, with an abundance of chintz and overstuffed furniture—just the type of place he would've expected Jenna to live. "The nursery is upstairs," she said.

Grady followed her up the stairs. "If you'll just get the door for me," Jenna whispered, "I'll put Andy down in his crib and then we'll talk."

"Sure." Grady wanted to talk, too. He stepped around her and opened the door. They stared at the room. It was completely empty.

"I DON'T BELIEVE THIS," Jenna muttered, distressed.

"Why am I not surprised?" Grady drawled, feeling his patience with the baffling turn of events fading fast. He had ruled out the practical-joke theory when he'd talked to Alec, but he hadn't ruled out a feminine-revenge plot. If it turned out Clarissa and Jenna were conspiring together to get back at him, he was going to be royally ticked off. Come to think of it, Jenna didn't look so happy herself.

She glared at him. "Don't tell me you're in on this, too!" she accused.

Grady frowned. "In on what?"

Jenna stalked past him with a glare and went to the master bedroom down the hall. While Grady lounged in the portal, she laid Andy down on the center of the bed. Taking pillows, she boxed the baby in a protective square to keep him from rolling off the bed, then covered him gently with a blanket.

Not wanting Andy to waken when so much still needed to be explained, Grady followed Jenna wordlessly downstairs and into the den she had converted into her foundation office. It had two computers, a copier, a fax machine and a three-line phone. Jenna jerked open the door on the desk and pulled out a manila file. To her relief, Andy's birth certificate was still inside. "Here," she said triumphantly. "Here it is."

The town listed on the birth certificate was Hudson Falls, New York, all right. The birth date listed was December twenty-sixth of the previous year. But the name on the birth certificate was not Jenna Sullivan. Grady gave Jenna a long-suffering look. "What is this supposed to prove?"

"That Andy is my child, of course."

Grady sat on the edge of her desk. His years as a cop had taught him to keep his emotions in check. "You're not Laura Johnson. Are you?"

"Of course not. That's just the name I gave the doctor in Hudson Falls."

Grady struggled for patience. "Why did you give the doctor a fake name?"

"Because I wanted Andy to be born to Laura Johnson so that Jenna Sullivan could adopt him. I've always wanted a child of my own to love. I've even thought about adopting. It wouldn't surprise anyone, least of all my family, to know I'd adopted a child. This way I figured I could spare my family from questions and gossip. This way, I figured, everyone would win, and no one would be hurt."

"Except the father, who didn't even know he'd brought a child into this world," Grady said heavily.

Jenna was silent. Suddenly, she looked every bit as guilty as Grady wanted her to feel.

He lowered his glance to the paper in his hands.

"Jenna, this birth certificate isn't legal," he pointed out with a great deal more calm than he felt at that particular moment.

"So?"

"If you based an adoption on a birth certificate that wasn't legal, then the adoption wouldn't be legal, either."

"So what? The adoption was all for show, anyway. Either way, Andy was my child. I was just trying to prevent him from bearing the brunt of any gossip."

Grady eyed Jenna contemplatively. Her logic had a sort of convoluted charm, made more appealing because all she had been trying to do was protect those she loved. Still, the day had been a long one, and Jenna was definitely showing the signs of it. Her thick, strawberry blond hair fell in rumpled waves to her shoulders. Her face was pale, her dark green eyes rimmed with fatigue. And yet there was something so sweetly vulnerable in the way she was looking at him that called forth a protective response from him that was ludicrous under the circumstances. For all he knew she was simply loony.

Grady sighed and folded his arms in front of him. "Let me get this straight. You had a baby here at home and put him in a nursery that does not exist—"

Jenna frowned. "The nursery did exist, until two weeks ago," she interrupted.

Grady decided to let that one pass. "Then you went into town and registered Andy's birth under a false name."

"And had him checked out by the town doctor. Don't forget that." She wagged a finger at him, adding, "He was in good health."

"What about you?"

Jenna's expression suddenly became closed and unreadable. "I'm fine," she said.

Sure you are, Grady thought. He cleared his throat. "You said you run across a lot of babies in your line of work?"

Jenna stiffened, knowing exactly where this line of questioning was leading. "I did not kidnap Andy from anyone else, if that's what you're implying," she said tightly.

In his years as a police officer, Grady had seen stranger things happen. "What about your ex-husband? Is there any chance this baby is his, or that he claimed the child he felt was his?"

Jenna glared at him as twin spots of pink appeared in her fair cheeks. "Unlike you, I do not make a habit of sleeping with my ex."

Deciding this conversation needed to be lightened up, pronto, before Jenna got hysterical on him, Grady feigned a blow to the chin. "Ouch."

"You deserved it," Jenna muttered under her breath. She lowered her glance.

Maybe, maybe not, Grady thought.

Jenna sighed. She circled the desk, faced him beseechingly. "Look, I can see you don't believe me," she began softly.

Grady had never been seduced into looking the other way when it came to anything illegal, and he wasn't about to start now. "Going on proof alone, there's not much reason I should," he said.

"Nanny Beth could tell you otherwise."

"If you knew where she was," Grady said, recalling that much from their previous conversation.

"She'll show up eventually," Jenna said confidently.

Jenna might not think her nanny was a suspect, but Grady had been trained to think more objectively. "Tell me more about Nanny Beth. How long have you known her?"

"As long as I can remember." Jenna pulled up a chair and sank into it. "She not only raised me from infancy when my mother died, but she stayed with me during my pregnancy and helped deliver Andy. I've always thought of her like a mother, and I daresay she thinks of me as her daughter."

Grady quirked a brow. "All the more reason she might want Andy to have a father and you a husband," he said thoughtfully.

Jenna leaned forward and unlaced her ankle boots. "Nanny Beth would never traumatize me like that," she said firmly. She curled her sock-clad toes several times and then stretched her long legs out in front of her.

Grady studied Jenna and tried to ignore the unconscious sexiness of her spread legs. "Are you sure?"

Jenna buried her face in her hand and barely stifled a yawn. "Yes."

"Was she here that day the baby disappeared?"

Jenna shook her head. Slouching a little lower in her chair, she stretched her arms wide on either side of her. "I told you before. She went into town to do some shopping."

"Before or after the baby disappeared?"

"Before." Jenna released a long breath, then got slowly to her feet. She bent and picked up her boots, carried them over to the doorway and set them down neatly on the other side of the portal. "I don't like the direction this conversation is headed, Grady," Jenna warned. She spun around, her back to the jamb, and regarded him patiently.

Grady found himself wishing she didn't look so sexy in the jeans and long, thigh-skimming sweater. "Too bad."

She kept her eyes on his and placed her hands behind her. "I told you before. I'll tell you again. Nanny Beth is not a suspect."

Grady decided it was high time he started taking notes. He whipped his notepad out of the inside of his tweed sports coat and turned to a fresh page. He wrote *NB* at the top of it. "And you say you haven't seen her since?"

Jenna continued to watch him, her face expressionless. "No."

"Was she scheduled for any sort of vacation?"

"No," Jenna said, "but that doesn't mean she wasn't persuaded to take one by one of my well-meaning relatives."

"The kidnapper," Grady said.

"Yes. It could be that Nanny was talked into cooperating."

"What if she didn't cooperate?" Grady asked. "Would anyone in your family hurt her?" Jenna shook her head. "Fire her?" Jenna paused. "I still want to put out an APB, just to make sure Nanny is okay," Grady said.

Jenna bit her lip, for the first time looking worried. "Could you do it in an unofficial way?"

Grady knew he shouldn't agree to this. But the silent plea for help in Jenna's eyes soon had him acquiescing. "All right. I'll call in a few markers. But if we don't find Nanny by the end of the week, we're going the official route."

Jenna nodded. "In the meantime, I'll look, too. I'll call my father and some of Nanny's friends, but that will have to wait until tomorrow morning."

Grady studied Jenna. Nanny Beth was like a mother to Jenna. She had been there for the birth of Jenna's baby and had left on the day of the alleged kidnapping. And then had simply left, unannounced, coincidentally while Jenna's baby was still missing? Something was out of place here. Ten to one, Jenna knew what it was. "None of this strikes you as odd?" he probed quietly.

Again, Jenna averted her gaze.

"What aren't you telling me, Jenna?"

"Nothing."

And pigs fly, Grady thought, but figuring he'd pushed her hard enough for one day, he said nothing more. He'd check out this nanny himself.

"Look, I'm exhausted. As much as I'd like to talk to Dr. Koen tonight, we can't really go to see him until morning."

"I agree." Grady paused. "Just to make sure no other mishaps occur while we're out here, the baby stays with me tonight," he said.

To his surprise, Jenna didn't argue, merely looked deep into his eyes. "You promise me you won't walk off with him?" she asked anxiously.

"I promise," Grady said softly.

"LOOK, JUST LET ME do the talking," Jenna said the next morning as Grady parked in front of Dr. Koen's office in Hudson Falls.

"I'll let you start," Grady agreed. He circled around to her side of the car, opened the door for her and helped her and the baby out. "I'm not promising not to ask any questions." He was ticked off enough that they were still unable to track down Nanny Beth, despite numerous phone calls on both their parts.

Jenna regarded him with obvious irritation. Her glance gentled. "Just don't embarrass me, okay?"

Grady frowned and didn't promise anything. As far as he was concerned, Jenna's story was implausible, at best. She did have one thing going for her, and that was the way Andy responded to her. Like the two of them were perfectly in sync. But then, as Jenna had pointed out the previous day, Andy had never really met an adult he didn't seem to like. He was such a cheerful, easygoing infant, he would've adapted to anyone, and Jenna had been fussing over him all morning.

To Grady's relief, the clinic seemed to be clean and well-run. The doctor who had allegedly taken care of Jenna was a young guy, in his late twenties. Probably fresh out of med school, Grady thought.

"Dr. Koen, this is Grady Noland. A friend of mine. It's a long, complicated story and I won't bore you with the details, but he'd like to ask a few questions."

"Sure." Dr. Koen gestured for both of them to take a seat.

Grady opened the manila file he'd brought in with him and slid it across the desk. "Were you the doctor that signed this birth certificate?"

"I sure did. This little guy was in such a rush to be born that Laura and her nanny delivered Andy all by themselves, out at that farmhouse." Dr. Koen grinned at Andy, who was snuggled contentedly in Jenna's arms. "They did a great job, too."

Grady resisted the urge to take out his pad and scribble a few notes. He could do that later. "When did you see them?" he asked.

"I got there shortly after the birth. I suggested Laura and her baby might want to go to the hospital at least for a day or so to rest and recuperate, but Laura was happy where she was, so I saw to her, made sure that she got the aftercare she needed, checked out the baby, wrote out the birth certificate, and that was pretty much that. Andy was due for his shots two weeks ago, you know."

"I know. I'm sorry," Jenna apologized. She smiled at Dr. Koen earnestly. "Things have been a little crazy. I'll take care of it."

"You can vouch that Laura here had a baby, though?" Grady asked.

Dr. Koen gave Grady an odd look, but answered anyway. "Oh, yes, there's no faking the aftermath of a birth." Dr. Koen paused. "Why do you ask?"

Grady shook his head. "There's been some confusion." Declining to reveal anything more, Grady stood, signaling the interview was over. He shook hands with Dr. Koen. "That's all the information I need for now." Grady paused to glance at Jenna, who was still studiously avoiding looking at either him or Dr. Koen. "But I may be back."

Dr. Koen cast Jenna a concerned look, then turned to Grady. "I'll be glad to be of any help I can," he said.

"Satisfied?" Jenna asked as they trooped out to the sidewalk.

Grady shook his head. "Not even a little bit." He wished to hell this mess could be cleared up so easily.

Jenna whirled on him. Her strawberry blond hair gleamed more red than gold in the morning sunlight. "Why not? He told you I had a baby."

"He also thinks you're Laura Johnson." Grady hustled Jenna and the baby toward the warmth of the car. "You've got a false name on the birth certificate. A nanny and a nursery full of baby furniture who've both disappeared. There are a lot of questions here, Jenna. A lot."

She swallowed and looked uneasy again as she got into the car, Andy still cradled in her arms. Grady circled to the driver's side. She watched him get in. "Where do you want to start?" she asked warily.

"With Nanny Beth, of course." Grady started the car and paused to let it warm up. "Do you think she could've taken the baby furniture out of your farmhouse?" Assuming, Grady added silently, there ever was any baby furniture there to begin with.

Jenna turned to him. "No, of course not."

"Then how and why did it disappear?"

Jenna bent her head and rummaged through the diaper bag for a bottle of formula a contented Andy didn't really need.

"Either you tell me or I'll find out myself," Grady threatened.

Jenna shot him an ominous look. "Must you play cops and robbers with my life?"

Grady told himself not to be distracted by the heightened color in her pretty face or the lively sparkle in her dark green eyes. "That all depends," he said silkily, watching as Jenna uncapped the bottle and tilted the nipple toward Andy's mouth. "Do you want to raise this child or not?"

She knew he meant it. She smiled at Andy, who was holding onto the bottle of formula with both hands while he nursed. "My father probably took the furniture."

Now they were getting somewhere, Grady thought with satisfaction. He worked to keep his expression impassive. "What makes you say that?"

Jenna studied the dashboard in front of her. "If you knew him, you wouldn't have to ask."

"Well, I don't know him," Grady grumbled, wishing Jenna hadn't worn that lavender perfume of hers.

Jenna glanced up to confront him. "I love him, okay? Get that straight first." Her chest rose as she drew in a deep breath. "But he's very overbearing and he hates scandal of any kind. At the first hint of any kind of scandal, he sweeps it under the rug."

Grady had known all along Jenna was holding something back. Now that they were edging toward it, his pulse began to race. "Did he know you were pregnant?"

"No."

"How'd you explain your weight gain?"

"I didn't. I didn't see him at all during that time."

Grady paused and began to feel uncertain again. "And he accepted that?" If Jenna's father was as protective as she seemed to indicate, the explanation didn't make sense.

Jenna shrugged. "He knows I'm as busy running my foundation as he is running Sullivan Shoes. Besides, we talk on the phone frequently, and fax each other almost daily, so it's not as if we're not in touch."

Grady wasn't one to dispute the value of a letter, phone call or fax. But there was something about being there in person, too. "What about Christmas?"

Jenna swallowed and began to look anxious again. "I told him I had to be in Sweden, on foundation business."

That made sense, if she hadn't wanted anyone to know about her pregnancy, Grady thought. He studied her relentlessly, in no hurry to leave now that they were sitting in the warm car. "When were you planning to tell him about the 'adoption'?"

"As soon as I was strong enough and had handled all the legal details," Jenna said briskly.

"Which would have been when?"

"About the time Andy was kidnapped, actually. I was just getting ready, mentally and emotionally, to tell him then. You know, rehearsing what I was going to say to him and all that."

"Not much of a liar?"

"Apparently not."

Silence fell between them. Grady wished she didn't look so damn vulnerable, as if he was the villain here, torturing her with his endless questions. Telling himself sternly to get back to business, to not let Jenna's sensitive nature affect him, Grady said, "Did you go to him when you realized the baby was missing?"

For a moment, Jenna was very still. "Yes," she said quietly.

"And?"

Jenna swallowed and lifted her head to meet his gaze. Twin spots of color appeared in her cheeks. "He was confused, to say the least."

"Then what happened?"

Jenna settled back in her seat and looked at the roof of the car. "You know, I really don't want to get into this."

Grady realized he was clenching his jaw. He sat back and made a concerted effort not to be so tense. "Why not?"

"Because my relationship with my family is none of your business, that's why. Besides, it'll all be cleared up in a few days, when the blood tests come in. Then you'll know Andy's my child and yours, and that'll be the end of it."

"Not quite," Grady said.

"What do you mean?"

"If what you've told me is true, Jenna, and I'll tell you again your story has more holes in it than a sieve, then our baby was kidnapped."

Jenna rolled her eyes in exasperation. This was not exactly news to her. "Great going, Sherlock. So what? He's safe now."

"But for how long?" Grady questioned impatiently. "Until we know for sure who took him and why, Andy won't be safe, Jenna, and neither will you."

For the first time in two days, she looked frightened. Her face paled. "What are you saying?"

"That I plan to continue this investigation until I get to the bottom of this mess." He didn't think Andy had been taken for ransom, but he couldn't be sure of it. And until he was . . .

Jenna started to look panicked, which made Grady suspicious again. What else hadn't she told him? She clutched his arm. "Grady, you can't—"

"I not only can, I will," he corrected with a ruthless, determined smile. He was going to discover the truth with or without Jenna's help. "And I'm going to start by talking to your father."

Chapter Four

"I don't understand why you have to talk to my father," Jenna said irritably as they entered her father's Albany, New York, home.

Grady stepped into the imposing front hall, Andy cradled in his strong arms. Jenna watched as Grady surveyed the luxurious interior of the home she had grown up in, taking in the gray-and-white marble floor beneath them, the sweeping staircase in front of them and the chandelier overhead. With only a passing glance at the formal parlor to their right, with its high ceilings, expensive Oriental rugs and glossy antiques, he handed her the baby and shrugged out of his trench coat. "For one thing, your father can verify your story about the baby being kidnapped on Valentine's Day."

"It wasn't a story," Jenna told Grady hotly as she handed him the baby and shrugged out of her own coat. "It was the truth!" Grady shifted the sleeping baby in his arms a little higher and gave her a skeptical glance.

"Why can't you just take my word?" Jenna whispered as she braced herself for the inevitably difficult confrontation with her father. He wasn't an unkind man. But he wasn't the easiest man to confide in, either. Even though she knew Lamar Sullivan loved her dearly.

Grady followed Jenna down the hall, past a wall of family paintings, to her father's study at the rear of the house. "I learned a long time ago to rely only on hard, cold facts." His voice was close, hushed. His warm breath brushed her ear.

Jenna swallowed, slowing her pace as they neared her father's study. She tilted her head to better study Grady's face. "In your police work, yes—"

He looked at her, his slate-blue eyes darkening decisively. "In my personal life, too," he said firmly.

Jenna drew in a jagged breath, aware her pulse had picked up marginally. "What does your heart tell you?" she asked.

"What my heart does or doesn't tell me is completely irrelevant," Grady said.

He looked so right, so natural, standing there with his baby in his arms. For a second, Jenna let herself fantasize about how happy an occasion it might have been, under other circumstances, if she and Grady had brought their baby home together to introduce him to the family.

Jenna released a wavering breath and knew a second's deep regret. If only she had never cooked up this ruse to begin with. If only she had been brave enough to be honest with everyone from the first, then she wouldn't be in this tangled mess that was bound, after their joint interview with her father, to become even more complicated and potentially damaging than it already was. Unless she could just prevail on Grady's goodness and get him to be on her side before they entered the study. She tilted her head a little farther and drew another, deeper breath. "Why can't you follow your heart, Grady?" she implored softly. *Please,* she thought, *just this once, put all the facts aside and just help me.*

He lifted his free hand to cup her face. "Because it's when I let my emotions get in the way of my thinking that I get into trouble, that's why."

His mesmerizing touch sent a blazing warmth into her skin. Determined not to be sensually distracted, Jenna stepped back and folded her arms in front of her. Her plan to save herself from further humiliation thwarted, her temper rose. "Well, I think that's ridiculous," she snapped.

Grady's gaze took on a lecturing quality. He stepped back, too. "Your emotions can only mess you up in a situation like this, Jenna," he warned flatly.

"I disagree," Jenna said. "Furthermore, I think you'd be a lot happier if you'd just let your heart guide you here."

Half his mouth curved up in a disbelieving smile. "And what do you think my heart is telling me?" he asked.

Jenna drew herself up straighter, so that the top of her head almost reached his chin. "It should be telling you to trust and believe in me, facts or no facts."

Grady sighed. "I can't do that."

She had been afraid of that. Jenna released a wavering sigh and shook her head in silent regret. "Then I can't be with you," she said.

"I don't recall asking you to be with me again," he pointed out dryly. But the sexual glimmer in his eyes said it was only a matter of time before he did.

"You'll get around to it, once you find out Andy really is your son," she predicted in a depressed tone.

He smiled at her again, looking just as intrigued, just as filled with a distinctly male satisfaction, as he had the night of Alec Roman's party. The night when this all began. "You think so?"

Her emotions in turmoil, she stared at him in silence. She wanted him to desire her again, just as she desired him. But she didn't want her life turning into a soap opera. She didn't want to risk losing her child.

Aware he was waiting for an answer from her, she finally nodded. "I know your type, Grady Noland."

"Do you, now."

"Yes, and unfortunately for me, you're noble to the core."

"Why is my being noble unfortunate for you?" he interrupted.

"Because," Jenna said, and felt her voice catch just a little. She swallowed hard, fighting back the tears she felt gathering in her throat and glimmering in her eyes.

"You'd die before you let the chance pass to do the right thing." Reaching for her baby, she gently insinuated her hands between his blanket-wrapped form and Grady's strong arm. Grady's body was taut with self-imposed control. "The trouble is, the right thing in this case is not destined to bring us anything but more heartbreak."

Grady released a long breath and jammed his hands on his waist. The action pushed back the edges of his gray Harris tweed sport coat, revealing the flatness of his abdomen beneath the starched light blue crispness of his oxford cloth shirt and the faded, soft, torso-hugging Levi's jeans. "You've got my life all planned out for me, don't you?" he accused cynically.

"I only wish," Jenna muttered. Finding his slate-blue glance a bit too probing, too knowing, for comfort, she turned away from him uneasily. She had an idea what he was thinking. It was as clear as the reluctant, wary expression on his face. The more he thought about her claims, the more ludicrous they sounded. The capper, of course, had been storming the nursery at the farm, only to find it empty. He had started to believe her up to then, at least to the point where he would humor her and investigate her claims. But now...now at least part of him thought she was a nut. Again.

In the study, footsteps sounded on the parquet floor. Her father came out into the hall. Lamar Sullivan's gaze went from Jenna and the sleeping baby in her arms to Grady, then back again. "Jenna." Briefly, he looked stunned.

Jenna knew exactly what he was thinking, too. She hoped she could count on her father's love of personal privacy to keep him from revealing too much to Grady about what had been going on in their family in the past few weeks.

Lamar cast a wary look at Grady. Frowning, he turned to Jenna. "What are you doing here? I thought you were still at Pinehaven—"

Damn, Jenna thought, Pinehaven was the one place she had not wanted mentioned in Grady's presence. She feigned nonchalance. "I decided to leave," she announced as if it was no big deal, when in fact it had been a very big deal.

Her father blinked. "They allowed that?" Lamar asked with a frown.

"Why should Jenna need permission to leave Pinehaven?" Grady interjected, obviously confused.

"Why else? I'm a very popular person," Jenna temporized quickly in a jovial voice, hoping she didn't look as utterly and completely panicked as she felt. *If Grady found out about Pinehaven, it really was going to be all over.* "It's not important. Dad, we can talk about Pinehaven later. I'm here to talk about Andy—"

"The baby," Lamar said slowly. Reaching behind him, he sank down onto the glossy antique parson's bench located just outside his study door.

"Yes, this is Andy, Dad. *You know, the baby I told you about when I was here a couple of weeks ago.*"

To Jenna's distress, Lamar paled even more. "Where did you get that baby, Jenna?"

Grady turned to Jenna suspiciously, his police antennae on full alert. "Yes, Jenna," Grady echoed her father pleasantly, his slate-blue eyes anything but innocent, "where did you get that baby?"

Jenna turned to Grady in irritation. He knew full well where she had gotten Andy. She gave Grady a quelling look, then walked over to her father. "It's a long story, Dad," Jenna said gently. She put her hand on Lamar's shoulder and looked into his eyes. "We can talk about it later." Her father nodded, picking up on her hint that not everything was supposed to be discussed in front of Grady. "In the meantime," Jenna continued smoothly, "I want to introduce you to someone. Grady Noland, Grady, my dad."

Recovering as quickly as she had hoped he would, Lamar got to his feet and shook hands firmly with Grady. "Grady, nice to meet you," Lamar said in the overly polite tone he used with strangers.

"Why don't we all go in your study," Jenna suggested.

"Certainly," Lamar said.

Once they were all cozily ensconced in the paneled room, Lamar behind his desk, Grady, Jenna and Andy in the twin leather wing chairs in front of it, Jenna continued much more confidently than she felt. "Grady wants you to verify something, Dad."

"What?" Lamar Sullivan said suspiciously.

Jenna pressed her lips together briefly and prayed for strength. She lifted her chin. "That two weeks ago, on the afternoon of Valentine's Day, I came to see you here at the house and told you I'd had a baby and that the baby had been kidnapped."

Lamar frowned at Jenna the same way he had when she'd gotten after-school detention for being late to class. His hands flat on the desk, he surprised her by turning to Grady. "You're going to have to excuse Jenna," he said kindly, following his reluctantly-voiced statement with a man-to-man glance. "She's not well. In fact, she was hospitalized recently for accumulated stress and emotional exhaustion." His dark green eyes gentled with sympathetic understanding. "Apparently, her divorce from Baxter was harder on her than all of us knew."

"Dad!" Jenna said.

"Well, it's true, honey," Lamar said gently. He got up from behind his desk and came around to stand beside her chair.

Afraid she would wake the still slumbering baby because she was so upset, Jenna got up and handed Andy over to Grady. "Look, we don't have to get into that right now," Jenna said sharply.

"Speak for yourself, Jenna. This is getting very interesting," Grady quipped.

Ignoring Grady studiously, Jenna turned to her father. She crossed her arms. Suddenly, everything was so much clearer. She didn't know why she hadn't seen it right away. It all made perfect sense. "You removed the nursery furniture from the farmhouse, didn't you, Dad?" *Because you thought I was crazy, too!*

"I don't know what you're talking about," Lamar said stiffly.

"Oh, no? Then what about Nanny Beth? I suppose you're going to say you don't know anything about *her* disappearance, either!" Jenna shot back hotly.

"Actually, I *did* have a hand in that," Lamar admitted quite freely. "I gave her a five-thousand-dollar bonus and sent her off on a much-needed month-long vacation. I could tell when I talked to her on the phone February fifteenth that she'd had her hands full, caring for you."

Jenna fought to keep control of her emotions. Only the fact that she knew she was responsible for at least part of what had conspired, and the fact that Grady was taking in everything, kept her from completely blowing up. "What did she say when you gave her the news?" Jenna asked, as serenely as possible.

Lamar shrugged and straightened his silk Perry Ellis tie. "She was worried about your being able to cope alone, of course. I told her we knew about the baby situation and that everything was under control . . . the family was taking care of you."

Which explained, Jenna thought, why Nanny Beth would have left her. She knew Jenna had been planning to tell her father about Andy the following day. She would have assumed Lamar Sullivan had welcomed both baby and daughter into his home. Nanny

Beth had left town never knowing Andy had been kidnapped, or that anything at all was amiss. "Where did she go?"

"I don't know. She said something about maybe taking a cruise."

"That's all you know?" Jenna asked, exasperated.

"Sorry," Lamar said.

"At least it's a start," Grady said. He looked at Jenna. "I'll call the station and have them start checking the cruise lines right away. With any luck, we'll find Nanny in a few days."

Jenna nodded and turned back to her father. Still trying to contain the damage and limit how much Grady was able to discover, Jenna gave her father a weary look laced with both gentleness and affection. "Look, Dad, I know things are a mess between us. A lot of it is my fault. I should have confided my troubles in you earlier, but I didn't. I can't go back and fix that now. Nevertheless, I'm asking you to trust me. There *really* was a baby, and Andy is that baby."

Lamar looked at the darling baby sleeping so peacefully in Grady's arms. "Is the baby Baxter's?" Lamar asked.

Jenna flushed to her roots. "Dad, please."

"I think that I have a right to know, since any child of yours is my grandchild," Lamar countered.

"Well, I'm not ready to tell you. When I am, I will."

"I see," Lamar said slowly, his expression thoughtful and intent. "What about Mr. Noland? Does he know who the father is?"

Jenna doubted her father was ready to hear about her fling with Grady, so she said simply, "Grady is a friend of mine, and a policeman. He has agreed to help me discover who took Andy from the farmhouse. He's as eager to get to the bottom of this situation as I am."

Again, Lamar frowned. He sat on the edge of his desk. "You called in the police?"

"Only in an unofficial capacity," Jenna soothed. Knowing that it was her family's loathing of any scandal that had precipitated this mess she was in now, Jenna looked her father directly in the eye. "There will be no public scandal if I can help it," she promised.

Lamar breathed an audible sigh of relief, then looked at Grady sternly. "Can you verify that this infant is my daughter's child?"

Grady shook his head, looking completely natural, sitting in the wing chair, the eight-week-old baby cradled in his powerful arms. "Not yet," he told Lamar, meeting the eyes of the man who under different conditions might have been his father-in-law. "Jenna took a DNA test, at her own request, but we won't have the results back for a few days."

"I see." Lamar's expression grew even more worried, heightening Jenna's dismay. "Can you verify for me this baby was actually kidnapped, then?"

"No, sir," Grady said, his frankness with her father unabating. "I can't."

Fierce emotion welled up within Jenna. She clasped her hands in front of her tightly, and worked to keep her voice low. "Dammit, Grady, you know he was." *You have to know that in your heart!*

But Grady only shook his head in calm disagreement, looking every bit the hardened city cop at that moment. "No, I don't," he said, as their eyes held and clashed. Jenna's heart pounded with equal parts fatigue and nerves. Maybe she should have told Grady about her brief hospitalization before coming here, and made him understand what a ridiculous mix-up it had all been.

Grady looked past Lamar to the family photos lining his desk. "No other grandchildren?" Grady asked, zeroing in immediately on the lack of infants or children in family portraits.

"No." Lamar frowned, making no effort to hide his disappointment in that to either Grady or Jenna. "My son, Kip, and his wife, Leslie, can't have any. Of course, Jenna here wanted children. But she was divorced, as you probably know, early last year, so—"

"Enough talk about my personal life, Dad," Jenna interrupted.

"I suppose you're right," Lamar said. "By the way, Jenna, your station wagon is still here."

Jenna nodded. "I'll drive my car back to the farmhouse when I leave today," Jenna said. "Grady and Andy can follow in his car."

An uncomfortable silence strung out between them, reminding Jenna of all that had been left unsaid. Grady still had a lot of questions.

Her father looked at Grady. "Is my daughter in any legal trouble here?" Lamar asked with a contemplative frown. "Does she need a lawyer?"

"As far as I know, there's nothing criminal going on that Jenna could be charged with," Grady said. Looking as restless as Jenna felt, he got up from the chair, Andy still in his arms, and began to pace the length of floor next to the bookcases.

Jenna turned away from Grady's tall, imposing form and back to her father. She knew Lamar loved her, even if he hadn't ever known quite what to do with her. "You swear to me you had nothing to do with that nursery furniture disappearing from the farmhouse?"

"I swear it," Lamar said softly, putting his hand over his heart. Without skipping a beat, he said, "You swear to me you're well enough to be out of the hospital?"

Their glances met and held. "Yes, Dad," Jenna said gently, "I am."

"Sir, if you wouldn't mind watching the baby for a few minutes," Grady said, interrupting them. His expression was intense enough to give Jenna pause. "I'd like to talk to Jenna alone."

Chapter Five

"I hope you're satisfied," Jenna grumbled cantankerously as she led the way to her old bedroom upstairs.

"Not yet," Grady drawled, "but I hope to be soon."

She raised a red-gold brow as he shut the door behind him. "You have completely shocked my father," Jenna complained.

"He's not near as shocked as he's going to be when he finds out you and I may have had a child together," Grady pointed out reasonably.

"We *did* have a child together, Grady."

He let that one pass and touched the quilted top of the frilly pink-and-white gingham bedspread. "This where you slept as a kid?" The canopy bed suited her somehow, he thought. In fact, the only thing he didn't like about imagining her in it was that it was a single.

"Yes. Not that it matters."

"You're right," Grady said, swiftly getting himself back on track. "We do have more pressing things to discuss, like precisely when you were hospitalized."

Jenna's spine stiffened. "I don't see why that matters," she retorted in a voice laced with pride.

Grady had expected a lack of cooperation on her part. "Fine," he said calmly, turning toward the door. "I'll just go down and ask your father to finish filling me in."

Jenna sprinted forward, closing the distance between them in three quick steps. She grabbed his arm. "All right, I'll tell you the whole story, but you have to promise me that you'll keep an open mind and not jump to any conclusions."

Grady tried not to let her touch, so soft and womanly, distract him. "Don't I always?" he said, holding himself very still.

Jenna dropped her arm. "Not so far, no."

He frowned. "Start talking, Jenna. I want to hear the details."

"I was admitted to the Pinehaven hospital around midnight on Valentine's Day."

"Is that here in Albany?"

"No, it's out in the country."

"Never heard of it," Grady said flatly.

"You're not supposed to have."

"Why not?"

Jenna shrugged again, her slender shoulders moving with enticing femininity beneath the jade cowl-necked sweater she wore over the long, flowing jade wool skirt. "It's extremely private, expensive."

Grady paused, Lamar's words ringing in his ears. *She's not well. In fact, she was hospitalized recently for accumulated stress and emotional exhaustion. Apparently, her divorce from Baxter was harder on her than all of us knew.* "And you agreed to this?" he asked slowly.

"Not exactly."

His muscles taut with the depth of his unease, Grady paced closer. He curved a hand against the side of her face, forcing her to look at him. "What does not exactly mean, Jenna?"

With a jerky motion, Jenna drew away from the warmth of his touch. Crossing her arms, she offered him her back. "It means I wasn't enthusiastic about the prospect," she replied through set teeth.

"But you agreed to be admitted anyway, knowing your son had just been kidnapped." Or was it *because* Andy had been kidnapped that Jenna had gone over the edge? Grady wondered. To accept that premise as gospel, he would have to take a lot on faith, maybe more than he was prepared to. And yet, something in him railed against the image of Jenna falling apart emotionally. Despite the feminine vulnerability in her nature, she seemed stronger than that. More determined, somehow.

Jenna whirled to face him, her jade wool skirt swirling around her in a drift of lavender-scented perfume. "Of course I didn't *agree* to be hospitalized!" she said angrily.

Grady blinked, a little taken aback by the depth of her emotion over this. "You just said—"

"You're not going to rest until you know the whole truth, are you?" Jenna demanded angrily.

"Probably not," he drawled. Feeling he might as well be comfortable, Grady sat down on the edge of her bed.

Jenna glared at him and continued to pace the length of the room. She waved her arms as she spoke. "When I couldn't find Andy, I was pretty upset, but I held it together until I got here. You see, initially I was sure my father was behind the kidnapping—"

"Why?" Grady interrupted with a frown. Having just met Lamar and seen how lovingly and protectively he treated his only daughter, Grady would not have come to the same conclusion.

"Because that's the way my father operates when he thinks I need protecting. He just charges in and does what he thinks is best for me. That's why I didn't tell him about the pregnancy. I was afraid he'd try to hunt down the baby's father. For my own good, of course." Jenna sighed.

"Is that the only reason you thought your dad had taken the baby?" Grady asked calmly.

"No. I knew my father had been worried about me living alone at the farm." Her eyes met Grady's. "My father had been asking Nanny Beth a lot of questions every time he called. I was afraid that Nanny Beth might have let something slip inadvertently, that my father might have discovered I'd had a baby somehow, reacted emotionally, and decided to do what the note had said and find Andy's father. I mean, it was such an old-fashioned, *male* thing to do, find the guy responsible for impregnating your daughter and make him pay up."

Grady admitted to himself that had it been his daughter he might have reacted the same way. "So when you drove into Albany that day and accused your father of kidnapping your baby, it was because you thought Nanny Beth had unknowingly clued your father in to what was going on with you," Grady said. "And that Lamar had acted the outraged father and taken it from there."

"Right," Jenna nodded. "Only I realized as soon as I started talking to my father that he knew absolutely nothing. Nanny Beth, bless her heart, hadn't clued my father in on a thing. And that, of course, meant my dad didn't have Andy, either...because if he'd had the baby, he would have admitted that to me and then given me a stern lecture on everything he thought I'd done wrong. But he didn't. Which in turn could've only meant one thing, that he didn't have Andy, either. And so I just totally freaked out."

Grady frowned. "Who did you think had the baby at that point?"

"I didn't know. That's why I wanted to call the police."

Grady felt himself being sucked in by her story, despite his initial cynical reaction to her claims. He struggled to remain as objective as he would in any police investigation. "And did you call the police that night?"

"No."

"Why not?"

Jenna swept her strawberry blond hair off her face. She looked aggrieved, remembering. "Because my father wanted to call Baxter first."

Grady paused, recalling Lamar's comment about Andy possibly being Jenna and Baxter's baby. Jenna had denied it vigorously. Grady still felt almost sick with jealousy at the thought. Struggling to put his emotions aside, he asked with a lazy indifference he couldn't begin to feel, "What does your ex-husband have to do with any of this, Jenna?" Was Jenna still in love with this Baxter?

"My father knows I'm not the type to have affairs, so he assumed my ex-husband was the father of any child I had. It only made sense that Baxter might have taken the baby, if he had somehow found out about my having a baby in secret."

"But you said Andy is our baby," Grady pointed out.

"Right," Jenna said. "Andy is our baby, Grady. But no one else knew that at that point, and I was so panicked I was willing to concede anything might have happened."

"Was there any other reason you suspected Baxter of the kidnapping?"

Jenna nodded. "One of the problems in my marriage was that Baxter, like my father, always felt that he knew what was best for me. And Baxter had been nosing around in my personal life, pursuing me... You see,

Baxter never wanted the divorce. So it made sense that if Baxter had found out about the baby, Baxter would have viewed the baby as an impediment to our getting back together and maybe done something about it."

"What happened when Baxter arrived?"

Jenna's lips thinned to a soft rosy line. "Baxter denied kidnapping Andy, or even knowing I'd had a baby."

Grady swallowed, hating to ask the next question, but knowing he had to. "Was there any chance it was Baxter's baby, or that he might have thought Andy was his child?"

"No."

"So why does your father still think it might have been Baxter's child?" Grady pressed.

Jenna was silent.

"Why does he think that, Jenna?" Grady repeated.

Jenna sighed. "Probably because of what else Baxter said to me that night," she said diffidently.

"Which was?"

"That we never should have gotten divorced. 'Clearly,' Baxter said, 'I wasn't meant to manage on my own and this just proved it.'" Just recalling the scene made her livid, Grady noted with satisfaction.

"What did you say to that?" Grady asked, resisting the urge to take Jenna in his arms and offer comfort.

"I told Baxter he was an arrogant jerk and I didn't want him trying to manage my life, from near or far."

Good for you, Grady thought fiercely. "How'd Baxter take that?"

Jenna released a shaky sigh. "He gave me a pitying look. My father looked like he wanted to sink through the floor—he hates emotional scenes, and this one was getting very bitter and recriminating."

"What happened next?" Grady said impatiently. Feeling a little edgy himself, he folded his arms.

Abruptly, she pushed away from the bed and began to pace again, her hands knotted into fists at her sides. "My father insisted I drink a little bourbon to calm down."

"And?" Grady stood and moved closer.

Jenna paused before the window overlooking the formal gardens, which were cloaked in a thin layer of dwindling winter snow. "I admit I felt like I needed a drink by that point, so I took the drink he gave me and went off to try to reach you again. Your buddies at the station said you were out working a case."

Grady remembered what he had been doing on Valentine's Day very well. "I was."

Jenna turned to face him. Her eyes leveled on his, and Grady suddenly found a great deal of feminine resentment heaped upon him. "Yeah, well, they made it sound as if you weren't," Jenna said tightly. "And that only upset me all the more."

"And then what happened?"

"It hit me... I mean, it *really* hit me that Andy was gone and I had no idea who had him, or even if he had actually been taken to you. So I started to cry and I couldn't stop." Jenna teared up, recalling. Her voice shook as she continued. "My father found me and became even more distressed because I was so completely distraught. Then Baxter left us alone, saying he would make a few phone calls to see what he could discover on his own about the baby. When Baxter returned, he said he had found some people who could help us figure out what was going on, and he wanted me and my father to go see them." Jenna took a deep breath and composed herself again. "*I* thought he meant detectives or something—Baxter meets all sorts of people, from his practice—and even though I suspected Baxter was just doing this to kiss up to me and my father and prove to me that I still needed him in my life, I said okay."

"Did you know what Pinehaven was?" Grady asked quietly.

"No." Jenna shook her head regretfully. "I'd never heard of Pinehaven. I could tell it was a hospital when we drove up." Remembering, Jenna began to tremble. "But I thought...well, I thought maybe Andy was there, that there had been an accident and Baxter knew about it because he was a doctor and had been calling the hospitals, to see what he could find out. So I went into the emergency room with them. We identified ourselves at the desk. And then a nurse took me to a room."

Grady was silent, absorbing the details of her story. If everything she was saying thus far was correct, then she had been through a real trauma. He took her hand in his and drew her to the canopied bed. He sat and guided her wordlessly to sit beside him. "When did you realize you were being checked in?"

"When they gave me a hospital gown to put on." Jenna's lips tightened mutinously. "I tried to leave, but they wouldn't let me. And as you can imagine, the more I insisted I wasn't crazy, the more they believed that I was."

"So your father just left you there even though you insisted you were fine?" Grady asked disbelievingly.

"He thought he was doing the right thing."

"I can't imagine why he would think that," Grady disagreed, "if you were even half as lucid as you are right now."

Jenna pushed away from the bed. Unable to sit still, she paced back and forth. "You have to put yourself in his shoes to understand. All Dad knew was that I had been acting strangely for months. Hiding out at the family farm, refusing to see anyone or even come home to spend Christmas with the rest of the family. Devoting myself entirely to my work, calling my childhood nanny out of retirement to act as my housekeeper. To make matters worse, I hadn't told him of either my pregnancy or Andy's birth. So when I finally showed up at his home on Valentine's Day and accused him of kidnapping a baby he hadn't even known I'd had, my father was *very* worried."

Put that way, Grady thought, it made sense that Lamar had acted as he had. "Worried enough to call Baxter," Grady surmised.

"Right. Dad trusted Baxter's medical expertise because Baxter is an excellent physician. And he trusted him with the confidentiality of the situation because Baxter was family, or had been."

Grady was quiet for a minute, thinking. It was true that hell had no fury like a woman—or man, in this case—scorned. "Do you think this could have been some sort of twisted plot for revenge on Baxter's part, a way of getting back at you or getting you under his control?" Grady asked quietly. Was this Baxter's way of seeking revenge on an ex-wife who no longer loved him?

"I don't know," Jenna said slowly. "Generally, Baxter is very straightforward in his attempts to control my life, but that approach wasn't working anymore."

"So you still consider Baxter a suspect in this, in your own mind?"

"Yes, I guess I do," Jenna said slowly. Her eyes were troubled as she looked at him. "But I also know if he did it, he didn't act alone. He was with me and my father at the very time Andy was left on Alec's doorstep."

"Any idea who might have been his accomplice?"

Jenna gestured helplessly. "The only other person who seems to have it in for me, at least openly, is your ex-wife."

"You think Clarissa and Baxter are in cahoots?"

Jenna was silent. "As far as I know, Clarissa and Baxter don't even know one another. But...I can't figure any other reason Clarissa would claim Andy was her baby, Grady, unless it's to keep us apart and win you back. And Baxter wants the same thing."

"But would Baxter really want to take your baby from you?" Grady asked.

"I'm not so sure that was the point of this, so much as to show me what a louse you are."

Grady showed his affront.

"Well, look at it from the kidnapper's point of view," Jenna continued. "For all he or she knows, you abandoned me, but foolish me, I was still pining away after you."

"Were you pining away after me?" Grady grinned.

Jenna flushed. Recovering, she shot him an arch look. "You'll never know."

Grady grinned again. Maybe there was hope for him and Jenna, after all. "I think we need to talk to Baxter," he said. "Do you know how to reach your ex-husband?"

Jenna nodded and gave Grady the number. Grady spoke to Baxter's secretary for several minutes. Finally, he hung up the phone. He felt frustrated, but he also knew they were making progress in the investigation. "Baxter's in surgery. He's got two operations scheduled, back-to-back. I've left word with his secretary that I want to see him first thing tomorrow morning to discuss you."

Jenna winced at Grady's choice of words. "He's probably not going to like that."

"Tough. I don't like my baby being kidnapped."

Neither had Jenna. The stormy look was back in her eyes. "I'd like to be there, too."

"Fine with me." Grady paused and reviewed his notes. "Okay, we've established a motive for Baxter kidnapping Andy, but we haven't established how he got your father to cooperate. How did Baxter convince your father that you needed to be hospitalized?"

"Easy. He just acted like the doctor he is and made a medical assessment of my behavior when my father requested his professional opinion."

Grady scowled. "Was this in front of you?"

"Heavens, no. If he'd done it in front of me, he never would have gotten away with it. It happened while I was off calling you at the station, Grady. While I was trying my hardest to get in touch with you, Baxter was telling my father that he thought one of two things had happened. I had either gone over the edge because of the divorce and my thwarted desire to have a child and had been suffering from a hysterical pregnancy—"

"An illness where a woman wants a baby so badly she imagines she's pregnant," Grady summarized.

"Right. Only in my case Baxter thought I'd taken it one step further than the average person and also imagined the birth and the kidnapping."

Grady had seen cases like that before, where women had wanted a baby so badly they stole someone else's...and then, through some mental aberration, came to believe it really was their own.

Jenna continued. "Or, Baxter theorized, it was possible I was just suffering a delayed reaction to the divorce and was simply emotionally exhausted and a little confused. All I needed was a few weeks of utter luxury and pampering, and someone to talk with me about my problems, and then I'd be back to my old self."

"And Lamar bought it," Grady guessed.

"As did the psychiatrist at Pinehaven Baxter talked to," Jenna affirmed furiously.

"How long were you in the hospital?" he asked casually.

Jenna's slender shoulders stiffened. "Why does that matter?" she asked as she messed with some of the antique silver picture frames on her dresser.

"It matters," Grady said, sensing she was evading again. "So answer the question."

She glared at him, resenting the third degree. "Two weeks," she said flatly.

Grady lifted a brow. One day he could understand, if she had been misdiagnosed, maybe even two—but two weeks! "Why didn't you get in touch with me and let me know?" he asked calmly.

"I tried to call you at the station the day after I was admitted."

Grady thought back rapidly and was immediately filled with regret. "I wasn't at the station on the fifteenth."

"I know," Jenna said. "I talked to your partner. He said you weren't coming in that day, that you'd called in and said something about a new baby in the family...and that you were taking time off to get acquainted with the little tyke."

"That was my sister's baby, not mine," Grady said, incensed.

"Yes, but I didn't know that," Jenna said, clasping her hands to her chest. "I had no idea until yesterday that Andy had ever been delivered to the wrong man at the wrong address. I thought the new baby you had told your partner about was Andy, that somehow someone had done what I never would've thought possible and gotten Andy to you. I asked your partner how you had sounded when you called in, and he said, 'Damn happy, but then Grady's always liked little kids.' He asked me if I wanted to leave a message if you called in again, and I said yes, and left my name and number at Pinehaven."

Grady regarded Jenna as she moved with angelic grace around the cozy bedroom. He wasn't sure whether it was a good sign or not, but this was all beginning to seem very plausible again. He could feel his guard letting down. "Did you explain to my partner that you were in a hospital?"

"I figured it was enough to leave the hospital number and try telling you one-on-one what was going on in my life, and with our baby. Only you never called back, Grady," Jenna said in a voice that was soft with accusation. She turned hurt eyes to him. "So I tried again and again. Each time you were out. I asked if you were still busy with the new baby, and your partner said, 'That and some family thing.' Your partner was also under the impression you had your hands full."

"I did," Grady confided ruefully. "My sister and her husband own a small ski lodge in Sun Valley. They've also got two other kids, both under six. She and her husband were pretty overwhelmed with everything. I went out to lend a hand at the front desk, help watch the kids, help take care of my new niece and get some skiing in. It was kind of a vacation and family reunion all in one."

"Sounds fun."

"It was." Only Grady didn't think he would have had any fun at all had he known what was happening to Jenna at the same time. Grady paused. "Did you leave another message for me?"

"Yes, the same one, several times. Again, my calls weren't returned. I figured you weren't calling me back as payback—because I hadn't told you about the baby. Finally, after about ten messages in three days, your partner explained to me that it was pointless to leave any more messages because you weren't calling in for them. If you had wanted me to know where you were, he said, you would've told me where you were going to be vacationing yourself. So if I wanted to talk to you, I was going to have to wait until you got back in town March first. So I comforted myself with the fact that you apparently had Andy and had welcomed him into your family, and perhaps wanted me to sweat it out awhile. I knew we had a lot to work out, you and I, but I figured it would wait until we could talk face-to-face,'' Jenna said. ''But you don't have to take my word on that, Grady. You can verify it simply by calling the station, checking your messages and talking to your partner.''

The part of Grady that had already loved Jenna told him it wasn't necessary to check out Jenna's story. The cop in him said it was. Wordlessly, Grady picked up the phone. A short talk with his partner later, he had his confirmation. To his enormous relief, everything was exactly as Jenna had said.

''Satisfied?'' Jenna said, when he hung up.

Grady frowned. ''There's something else I still don't understand.'' And it was a biggie. ''If you weren't sick, why did you stay in the hospital two weeks? Why weren't you able to get released right away?''

''I wasn't exactly what you'd call a model patient, going in,'' she admitted reluctantly. ''I was very upset about being admitted over my protestations that I was not crazy, and I tried to escape a couple of times.''

In her place, had he been incorrectly diagnosed and locked up in a psychiatric facility, Grady probably would have done the same thing. ''Couldn't they tell you'd just had a baby?'' he asked, fighting to put aside his empathy and retain his objectivity.

Jenna made another helpless gesture with her hands. ''After six weeks, my body was entirely healed.''

Grady forced himself to ask the questions he desperately needed answered, even though he knew they were a major invasion of her privacy. ''How do you know?''

Irritation flashed in her jade eyes. "Because I had just had my six weeks postpartum check-up the day before Andy was kidnapped."

"There must've been some signs you'd just had a baby," Grady said.

Jenna fixed him with the sort of smile a saleswoman reserves for her most difficult customers. "Maybe, if I'd still been nursing, but I had stopped that after four weeks," she said coolly. "So I had no milk in my breasts, either."

"Still, there must have been other signs," Grady persisted.

"Right." Jenna leaned toward him, her aggravation apparent. "And every single damn one of them worked against me!"

Grady narrowed her eyes. "What do you mean?"

Jenna rubbed at the back of her neck. "To be perfectly frank, Grady, I was a wreck. I was run down, emotionally and physically. I hadn't been sleeping enough, so I had circles under my eyes. I hadn't had enough exercise. I was still carrying ten extra pounds. And I was fighting the usual postpartum depression. I know, on the surface at least, that I must have looked like I was in terrible shape—at least compared to the pulled-together way I usually looked, pre-pregnancy."

Grady couldn't imagine Jenna ever not looking beautiful. Even now, with her strawberry blond hair in windswept disarray, her cheeks flushed with the heat of her humiliation and rage as she described all she had been through, her lips bare of any lipstick, she looked incredibly desirable. Incredibly womanly. And in charge of herself. So in charge of herself, in fact, he was having trouble believing she had ever not been in total control.

Grady paused. "Didn't your family know you were okay, though, when they talked to you the next day or the day after that?"

Jenna's fingers gripped the top of the dresser on either side of her. "My father would have, had he been allowed to talk to me."

Grady focused on her hands, with their neat unpolished nails, slender fingers and soft white skin. "But Lamar wasn't allowed to talk to you," he guessed.

"That's not so out of the ordinary, Grady. Initially I was very angry with Dad and Baxter for checking me into that place," she explained pragmatically. "I was not exactly shy about making my feelings known. The staff concluded seeing my family would only upset me further, so they asked them not to visit for the first couple of weeks. To keep track of my progress by phone calls to the doctor, instead."

Grady recalled the photos he'd seen on Lamar's desk. "What about your brother? Was he a part of this?" Was there a disputed inheritance at stake?

"Kip and his wife have been vacationing in Hawaii. I'm not sure Kip knows even now I ever was hospitalized."

"Your father wouldn't have told him?"

Jenna shook her head firmly, sure about this much. "There was nothing Kip could have done except worry, and my father was already doing enough of that for both of them, I'd wager. So he probably just decided to tell Kip when Kip and Leslie got back from Hawaii."

Grady released a heavy sigh. "Back to your stay in the hospital. What happened after that first night? I mean, I assume you saw a doctor—"

"Yes, and I demanded she let me out of there, pronto, so I could contact the Philadelphia police and find my baby. As you can imagine, that was probably the worst thing I could've said, since she initially thought I was suffering from a hysterical pregnancy and possibly delusions of motherhood. She didn't believe I'd had a baby any more than my ex-husband or my father did."

"Did she try to verify the birth anyway?"

"Yes, she checked with Dr. Koen in Hudson Falls. But I was so upset I forget to forewarn her that I'd had the baby under a false name, so all she discovered was that someone named Laura Johnson had allegedly been staying at my address and had had a baby. Finally, the second day we faxed Dr. Koen a photo of me. He verified that the woman in the photo was Laura Johnson, and that's when the tide began to turn in my favor."

"So what happened next?"

Jenna shrugged again. "I tried to reach you through the department, and that's when I learned you had the baby...at least I thought you had the baby. But you didn't return my calls. I was afraid to leave Pinehaven by then, for fear you'd try to get in touch with me in the interim and then we'd miss each other. And I didn't know where either you or Andy were. So I stayed another day. The third day I learned you weren't coming back with Andy for a couple of weeks, so I thought about everything that had happened and I weighed my options. I realized that I *was* incredibly run down and burned out emotionally from the stress of dealing with an unplanned pregnancy while simultaneously trying to hide out from the world and juggle the demands of the work I love. I decided to stay at Pinehaven and make good use of the opportunity to get my thoughts in order and my strength back before I tried to deal with you face-to-face and tackle single motherhood again.

"So I ate and slept and exercised . . . and slept and slept. And I talked to my doctor about the emotional pressure I'd been under, and the fact that I really hadn't been handling it as well as I thought I was."

"And so your stay in the hospital helped?" Grady asked.

"A lot," Jenna confirmed honestly. She shrugged. "On the whole, except for the rocky beginning, my stay at Pinehaven wasn't all that different from going to one of the plush rejuvenating spas. Of course, it would've been a different situation entirely had I suspected, even for a second, that Andy was not with you. But I really thought Andy was with you and everything was okay. That it wasn't going to make any difference if I came back sooner, because in or out of Pinehaven I probably wasn't going to get Andy back from you any quicker, and what I really needed to do was pull myself together, which I did."

Yes, she had, Grady thought. In fact, everything Jenna had done thus far was beginning to make sense to Grady. Too much sense for his own comfort. He was supposed to be objective and impartial here, but he had hardly given a thought to Clarissa's claims. And that wasn't like him. Usually he was thorough and impartial to a fault. "When did you get out of Pinehaven?" he said.

"Yesterday. I timed my release for the day you'd be back in Philadelphia."

Grady thought of Lamar Sullivan's reaction when his daughter had walked in the door. "And yet your father didn't know you'd been released?"

"I specifically asked my doctor not to talk to either Baxter or my father about the fact I'd really had a baby or was being released until I'd had a chance to talk to you and clear things up. My doctor understood I had been unfair to you, that I wanted to rectify that. As soon as I was released, I rented a car and drove straight to Philadelphia to see you."

Grady hesitated, aware he had never heard a crazier string of events explained more logically in his life. He was also aware he wanted very much for every word Jenna had said to be true.

"If all this is true, then you've been through a lot," Grady said. And for that alone, his heart went out to her.

She regarded him hesitantly, then sat down beside him on the bed, so close they were almost touching. She took his hand in both of hers. "Enough to make you stop doubting me?" she asked softly.

It still bothered Grady that Lamar Sullivan hadn't had any idea his daughter was pregnant. It also bothered him that Clarissa was claiming this baby, too. "*If* Andy's yours—" he began cautiously.

Jenna dropped his hand. "If?" She stood and looked at him as if he was a serial killer.

Grady released an exasperated breath. "What do you want me to say, Jenna?"

Without answering him, she set her lips firmly and started to step past him. Not about to let her run away, Grady stood and fastened an arm around her wrist and pulled her beside him.

Furious at the way he held her still so effortlessly, she glared up at him, the full brunt of her temper shining in her dark green eyes. "Let me go."

"No. Not until we've settled things, and we haven't finished talking."

"This isn't fair, Grady," she said angrily.

Grady tightened his hands on her wrists and felt the smooth, warm burn of her silky skin against his. Desire welled up deep inside him as his eyes locked on hers. "I'll tell you what isn't fair," he returned, not bothering to hide his resentment any longer. "The way this whole thing has unfolded, bit by incriminating bit. I don't like being played for a fool, Jenna. I don't like finding out by accident that I've brought a child into this world!"

Guilty color illuminated her cheeks, bringing out the delicate aristocratic bone structure of her face. "Well, what did you expect?" she ground out, struggling to free herself, to no avail.

Grady fought the potent desire that seemed to increase with every twitch and flail of her slender body. "Maybe the truth, the whole truth and nothing but the truth right from the start," he stormed, still holding her close.

Her eyes flashed with temper once again, then shone with hurt. "And how was I supposed to deliver that?" she whispered emotionally. Her soft, bow-shaped lips tightened in misery. "I didn't even know if you cared."

Grady ignored the guilt her words roused and concentrated only on all *he* had lost. Witnessing the birth of his first and only child. Being there for her when she needed him. "I cared, all right," he said, his low voice gruff with hurt. "You just never gave me a chance to show you."

With a sweep of her thick red-gold lashes, Jenna averted her eyes. "Maybe about the child," she asserted, "not about me."

Grady felt his temper rise another notch. "That isn't true!"

"Isn't it?"

"No!"

"Then why didn't you ever call me?" Jenna cried.

She had a point there. What she didn't know was that he had thought about calling her, countless times, and never more than when he'd been in Sun Valley with his sister and her family. Because it had been brought home to him, like an arrow to his heart, how much he was missing by not having a family of his own. He had begun to rethink his decision never to marry again. And once that decision had started to fall by the wayside, the first—hell—the only woman that had come to mind was Jenna. But he knew to tell her that now would sound like a damn lie.

"You're right. I should have called you, Jenna." He searched her eyes with his, saw the softness, the hurt, the feminine mystery that was all Jenna. Giving in to instinct, he lowered his mouth to hers. "I really should have," he whispered.

She had time to evade, if she had wanted to do so, but she didn't. She merely stared up at him with a mixture of wide-eyed wonder and wariness that made Grady feel all the more tender and protective of her. His lips caressed hers, gently this time, wonderingly. For a moment, Jenna was very still. Then she moaned low in her throat, and her arms came up to wrap about his neck. The next thing he knew she was kissing him back, not just in surrender but with an urgency that rocked him to his soul.

Passion for passion, he met her needs with his, met her desire, matched it over and over until his blood began to swim, until he knew it was either call a halt or take her then and there. He slowly ended the kiss and lifted his mouth from hers.

They sighed in unison. Both were trembling, dumbstruck. And cautious as hell. She was the first to turn away. She shook her head at him, as if silently chastising them both, swallowed hard, then slowly returned her gaze to his. "You shouldn't have done that," she said.

"*We* shouldn't have done that," he corrected.

Her face paled even more. Ducking her head again, she toyed with a button on his shirt. "Oh, Grady. Don't you see you're just confusing things more, kissing me that way?" she whispered.

Grady tucked a hand beneath her chin and guided her face to his. He knew it was crazy, that it was likely to complicate his investigation unnecessarily, but part of him just didn't care. "Or maybe I'm just clearing them up," he said. He knew, whether she wanted to admit it or not, that she desired him, too. The way she had kissed him just now proved that. And he had missed her, even if he couldn't tell her so just yet.

Jenna's soft lower lip took on a determined pout. "The desire we feel for one another doesn't matter, not unless you believe in me," Jenna asserted stubbornly, her slender body growing defiantly taut all over as she glared at him hotly. "Not unless you know in your heart that every single word I'm telling you is the truth, whether I have any proof to give you or not!"

His lower body throbbing with unslaked desire, Grady paused. She was asking him to disregard the statements and actions of everyone else and to believe only her. Sadly, he couldn't do that, not until he'd had a chance to discover and sift through all the facts at length. "All I know for certain is that I still want you," he said gruffly. "And I'm beginning to think I always will."

Wanting to explore more of what she had just given him, he lowered his mouth to hers once again.

"Don't." Jenna flattened a hand against his chest and pushed him away.

Grady let her hold him at bay, at least for the moment. "Why not?" he asked, his heart racing, need flowing through him like a river as he tested her once again. "I thought you just said you wanted me to act on my feelings."

"Only in order to help me," Jenna specified defiantly. "Not to get me in trouble again."

Unable to help himself, Grady sifted his hands through the soft waves of her hair. "You call this trouble?" Compared to what they had already been through, it was nothing.

Jenna shrugged off his touch and regarded him cantankerously, the desire she felt reflected in her dark green eyes. "You're telling me it's not?"

Chapter Six

"There you two are! I thought you'd never get back!" Clarissa said.

Jenna and Grady got out of their cars. Jenna took charge of Andy and Grady took charge of the diaper bag. They met Clarissa on the front porch of the farmhouse. "How did you know we were in Hudson Falls?" Jenna asked Clarissa warily, being careful to keep Andy's face turned away from the brisk March wind. She had hoped to avoid another scene with Clarissa until after the results of the blood tests came in. After that, well, there wouldn't be much to say. Clarissa's ruse would be discovered.

"Grady left your number and address with the Philly police department," Clarissa said smugly, looking exceedingly pleased with herself for having been able to track them down.

Jenna gave Grady a look. "How thoughtful of you to make sure Clarissa knew where we could be reached at all times," she said sweetly.

Grady knew Jenna well enough to read between the lines. "I left the number here so they could reach me if they came up with anything on Nanny Beth," Grady explained to Jenna. He turned to his ex-wife with a frown. "But that doesn't explain how you got that information, Clarissa. I know you didn't get it from my partner."

"I told one of the rookies it was a family emergency," Clarissa admitted cavalierly. Grady's look narrowed even more. His disapproval was palpable. Clarissa finally had the grace to blush. "Oh, for heaven's sake, Grady," she said, "we were married!"

"*Were* being the operative word, Clarissa," Grady said shortly. "We aren't now."

"Yes, but we should be," Clarissa continued, "for our baby's sake."

Holding on to her temper, Jenna punched in the code to deactivate the alarm system. Keeping her dignity wrapped around her like an invisible armor that would protect her from Clarissa's lies, Jenna stepped wordlessly inside, Andy cradled in her arms. Grady and Clarissa followed her as Jenna switched on lights and paused beside the thermostat in the hall to turn up the heat.

All but ignoring the baby she claimed was hers, Clarissa shrugged out of her mink. Her discreetly colored blond hair was a shining cap around her head. "I brought the papers you wanted, Grady."

A cold chill spread from Jenna's stomach into her limbs. She had known in her heart Clarissa wasn't going to give Grady up without a fight. "What papers?" Jenna asked warily.

Clarissa moved in on Grady, her expensive perfume dominating the air around her. As Jenna and Andy watched from the sidelines, Clarissa pressed a manila file full of official-looking papers into Grady's hands. "Birth certificate. Signed, notarized affidavits from the doctor and nurse who attended Andrew's birth. Now that you have them, Grady, I demand that we reconcile at once for the baby's sake."

Jenna had never considered herself a very physical person. In fact, she'd gone through her entire childhood without once getting into a brawl, but suddenly it was all she could do to keep from socking Clarissa in her turned-up little nose.

As if reading Jenna's intentions, Grady stepped between the two women. "It's a bit more complicated than that, Clarissa. Jenna has a birth certificate for Andy, too."

Clarissa looked stunned at the news. "Then hers must be a fraud," she said coolly.

"As a matter of fact, it is." Grady opened the file of documents Clarissa had handed him and scanned them quickly, one after another. If he found anything amiss in them, Jenna realized with fast-growing desperation, it didn't show in his face.

"Then what are you waiting for?" Clarissa demanded.

"The whole story," Grady said. He shut the file decisively but did not hand it to his ex-wife. "For all I know, your documents are false, too, Clarissa."

Jenna held Andy a little closer to her chest. Ducking her head, she drank in the sweet, baby scent of him. She had missed him so much, the two weeks they were apart. There was no way anyone was going to separate the two of them again, and she didn't care who she had to mow down to protect her relationship with him. Andy gurgled and cooed as Jenna pressed a kiss on the top of his soft, downy hair. She caught Grady watching her, a speculative gleam in his slate-blue eyes.

"Those documents are definitely false," Jenna said flatly, unable to help herself from putting in her own two cents worth.

Clarissa curled an elegant hand around Grady's bicep. "Don't take her word for it, Grady," Clarissa put in quickly.

Jenna's temper simmered as she saw how possessively Clarissa was holding on to Grady. Like they couldn't do that somewhere—anywhere—else!

"I don't intend to," Grady told Clarissa. He extricated her hand from his arm and stepped away. "Any more than I intend to take yours." Grady looked at his ex-wife like a prosecuting attorney about to put a hostile witness on the stand.

Jenna watched as Grady ushered Clarissa into Jenna's office.

"Have a seat, Clarissa," he told his ex-wife with a dissecting smile that didn't reach his eyes. "As long as you're here, I want to ask you a few questions, too."

GRADY WAITED until Jenna had gone off to heat Andy's formula before he settled on the desk and spoke to Clarissa. He had heard Jenna's story in all its crazy entirety. He had seen her substantiating paperwork. He had seen Clarissa's. Both of them couldn't be telling the truth. Frowning, he began, "First of all, I want you to know, Clarissa, that if this is some sort of ploy to get even with me or punish me for divorcing you, it wore thin a long time ago."

Clarissa crossed her legs at the knee. The slim, short skirt of her silk dress rode halfway up her thigh. She made no effort to pull it down. "I'm surprised at you, Grady," she scolded in a low, throaty tone. "I never would've imagined you to be the kind of man who'd think fatherhood was a punishment."

Grady wondered how he ever could have married Clarissa. It was clear she was not, and had never really been, his type. He supposed it had just been his age—he'd been right out of college—and his hormones that had done him in. He'd wanted to sleep with a woman every night. That woman had been Clarissa. Now that he really knew her, knew how bankrupt her soul was, he couldn't imagine ever being in love with her. Worse, the thought she might have had his child to trap him filled him with dread.

He scowled at her and forced himself to get back on track. "Fatherhood isn't a punishment," he said, scowling even more.

"Good." Clarissa sat back in her chair and let her skirt hike up a little more. "We agree on something."

Grady studied her pretty profile. "How could you have had a child and not told me, Clarissa?" Despite everything she had said, he just couldn't imagine her being brave enough to have his child without him. Oh, he remembered the story she had told initially, about running to her family on Long Island to have her baby. He just didn't buy it. It seemed to him she would have come to him first. Unless she really was intent on punishing him. And maybe, Grady thought sadly, she was.

Clarissa ignored the skepticism on his face. "I was angry with you for telling me in no uncertain terms it was over between us after you'd slept with me again, instead of before," she explained. "I was angry with you for insisting on going through with the divorce when you knew I still loved you. And initially I was not thrilled to find myself pregnant."

Grady recalled how Clarissa had refused to have his baby while they were married. Initially, she had kept putting him off, saying they would have a family when the time was right. It was only as they approached their thirties that she leveled with him and told him she had no interest in being a mother, period. "I remember how you felt about not having children," he said flatly. "So what changed your mind?"

"Nothing changed my mind. My getting pregnant was an accident. Furthermore, if you'll just think back to the night it happened, the night my place got burglarized, the night before we signed the final papers, you'll understand how and why I might have been so careless as to let something like this happen. I was very frightened, and you comforted me."

Grady sighed, unable to mask his regret about that. "I remember," he said tersely. Clarissa had been upset as hell that night, and not just about the burglary of her apartment, but about everything. He'd felt many of the same emotions she had. He had never failed in anything, either. He wasn't happy about failing in his marriage. And he felt guilty as hell for hurting Clarissa, because he knew he never should have married her. He just didn't love her enough, not the way a husband should love his wife. So when Clarissa reached out to him one last time, he'd just said the hell with it and let himself be seduced that one last time. Only he'd felt more alone and lonely after their lovemaking than he had when they'd first split. And he had also known that, no matter how many guilt trips Clarissa laid on him, he could never love her again. Andy didn't change that, even if he was their child.

"That night was a mistake, Clarissa," Grady said heavily, wishing it was possible to somehow discourage Clarissa once and for all, to let her know it truly was over, without hurting her feelings or enraging her.

Clarissa plucked at the silk fabric of her skirt. "I felt that way then, too, Grady."

"We agreed it would never happen again."

"Yes." Clarissa bit her lip. "But that was before I spent the last year alone." Suddenly, she was on her feet, her arms outstretched, moving toward him. "I want you back," she whispered.

"Then take him," Jenna interrupted from the doorway. Andy was no longer in her arms, so Grady concluded she had fed and changed the baby and then put him down in his crib. "Just don't use my baby to try and trick him into it."

Clarissa sent Jenna a wickedly derisive look, then turned to Grady. She ran her hand up and down his arm. The only effect it had on Grady was to make him want to pull away.

"Look, Grady, I admit I have made some mistakes, but it's silly to let my pride or yours get in the way of our being a family again," Clarissa said softly. As she looked at him, her eyes sparkled with an earnest glow. "I can handle this unexpected excitement in our lives, and I know you can, too."

Grady calmly extricated Clarissa's fingers from his arm and pointed to the chair. "Sit down, Clarissa, and finish answering my questions. How did the baby get to Alec's?"

Clarissa flounced to the chair and sat down, letting her skirt hike up even higher this time. "I told you," she pouted, swinging one crossed leg as Jenna walked over to collect the stack of unopened mail that had collected on her desk. "I left him there when I couldn't contact you. I just never imagined Alec or Jack would claim Andy as their own. I figured Alec would call you right away. And once you saw Andy, you'd realize the resemblance, you'd know..."

Jenna whirled to face Grady's ex. Her cheeks and eyes were aglow with fiery temper. "She's lying!" Jenna said.

Clarissa arched an elegant brow at Jenna. "One of us is," she agreed coolly.

Jenna's jaw clenched. "This is my home," she announced flatly, "and I didn't invite you here."

"Don't pretend you're an innocent." Clarissa got out of her chair and advanced on Jenna. "You're just after Grady's money," she accused.

Bull, Grady thought. Jenna turned to Grady, her surprise evident. "I didn't know you were wealthy," she said.

"I'm not," he replied, wishing Clarissa hadn't brought that up.

"But his family is very wealthy," Clarissa said.

"Well, so is mine," Jenna retorted with a harumph. "I'm an heir to Sullivan Shoes."

Clarissa turned to Grady. Her theory shot to hell, she demanded of him impatiently, "How much longer are you going to let this nonsense go on, Grady?"

"Until we get the lab results," Grady said, "or someone owns up to the truth and admits they've lied here or been playing a practical joke that ceased to be funny two days ago."

"Why do we have to wait?" Clarissa demanded petulantly.

"Because," Grady said, "this situation is far too complicated for me to trust anything less than the DNA results."

Clarissa released a long sigh. She turned to Jenna with a look that seemed to say, don't think you've won here. Wordlessly, she collected her signature white mink and her purse. "Grady, I'm staying at the Americana Inn in Albany. I've also reserved a room for you there." She paused in the portal to give Grady a smoldering look that had absolutely no effect on him, but made Jenna livid. "I'll be waiting for you," she cooed.

Bloody hell, Grady thought. Wordlessly, he helped Clarissa with her coat and walked her out to her car.

"SO. HOW WAS the good-night kiss?" Jenna asked the moment Grady strolled masterfully in the door a good ten minutes later.

"I didn't give her one." He paused, looking her up and down from the top of her mussed strawberry blond hair to the toes of her boot-clad feet. Still eyeing her with a depth of male speculation Jenna found greatly disturbing, Grady shifted so he stood with his feet braced slightly apart. He jammed his hands on his hips and narrowed his eyes. "Why would you think I had?"

"Oh, I don't know," Jenna replied with a lofty wave of her hand. She turned on her heel and started for the kitchen. With Andy sound asleep, now was the perfect time to start dinner. "You kissed me today. I just thought, to be perfectly fair, you'd also want to kiss Clarissa, too. You know, kind of a sampling-the-merchandise type thing, like one of those taste tests you see them doing in the grocery store on TV."

He caught her by the arm and yanked her forward until she collided with the hard muscles of his chest and abdomen. Sparks of sexual electricity exploded at every point of contact. "I don't operate that way, Jenna," Grady said.

Jenna's pulse pounded as she realized he looked like he wanted to kiss her. It was all she could do not to give in to impulse. "Really?" Jenna pushed away from him and offered him her back. "You could have fooled me."

Grady rested both palms on her shoulders. He ducked his head until it was close to her ear. "Why are you so angry at me?" he murmured.

"I don't know," Jenna said stubbornly. She tried to pull away. This time he wouldn't let her. She forced herself to go on. "Maybe it has something to do with the fact that I finally worked up enough nerve to tell you the truth, and it hasn't seemed to make a damn bit of difference."

Grady dropped his hands from her shoulders abruptly. He moved toward the kitchen sink. "I admit it's a very compelling story, very creative." He glanced out at the black night, turned to her slowly and folded his arms in front of him. "But then so is Clarissa's."

Jenna charged right after him. "I didn't tell you a story, Grady!" she said, hearing with chagrin the frustrated fury in her voice. "I told you the truth!"

"Then the facts will bear that out, won't they?" Grady retorted calmly.

Jenna glowered at him. She could feel the blood rushing to her cheeks, even as she struggled to get a handle on her soaring emotions. "Get out of my house." That said, she pivoted smartly on her heel and made for her study. Maybe if she did some work tonight, she'd be able to calm down.

As she feared he might, Grady intercepted her at the door. A sexy smile on his face, he braced a hand on either side of her and leaned over her. "If you want me to go, I'll go, but I'll have to get someone out here to watch over you and Andy first."

Jenna backed up slightly. Her heart was pounding. She was tingling all over. She told herself it was the tension causing her body to go haywire, and not his proximity. "Why?" she ground out. She let him know with a single glance she'd about had it with him.

Grady only leaned in closer. "Because if you are telling me the truth and Andy was kidnapped, then it could happen again, couldn't it? Particularly here."

Jenna swallowed, her adrenaline pumping for a completely different reason. "I think I hate you."

Grady grimaced right back at her. "If you had my baby without me, then I'm damned mad at you, too."

Wordlessly, Jenna slipped away from him. Refusing to address what she had no excuse for, she picked up the threads of their argument. "Furthermore, your ex-wife is a witch on wheels."

Grady grinned, amused by the apt description. "When I married her Clarissa was sweet and innocent and had stars in her eyes."

That didn't sound like the woman Jenna had met. "So what did you do to make her bitter?"

Grady's face changed. Some of the anger came back into his eyes. "I stayed a cop."

Jenna stared at him, her heart still pounding, aware she'd touched a nerve. And yet, as mad as she was with him, she still wanted so badly to understand him. "I don't get it."

Grady shrugged and shoved his hands through his agreeably shaggy mane of sable brown hair. "Clarissa always considered my police work nothing more than a rich boy's whim. She married me, sure I would grow out of it and take my rightful place in my father's brokerage firm on Wall Street."

Jenna studied his tall, lanky form. There was nothing soft or easy about Grady Noland. She sensed there never would be. He was who he was, take him or leave him. Trying not to think how much they had in common that way, Jenna asked, "You never even thought about quitting—for her?"

"Nope." Grady's answer was firm and unapologetic. "Nor do I ever intend to. I'm a cop, Jenna," he said. "It's what I do and what I am, and that's never going to change."

Jenna released a slow, slightly ragged breath. It was crazy, but it reassured her, knowing that Grady was so solid inside, so sure of himself and what he was meant to be. Now if only he wasn't so sure he was meant to go through this life alone. She decided to test the waters delicately. "The night we met, you said cops and marriage don't mix."

For the first time that night she saw a hint of remorse in Grady's eyes. "I still believe that in most cases," he said expressionlessly. Their glances met and held.

"Why?" Jenna asked softly.

Abruptly, Grady looked like a trapped panther pacing his cage. "It's a dangerous job. Long hours. Low pay." He moved his broad shoulders beneath his trademark Harris tweed jacket and finished, "All that combined is hard on a wife."

Jenna frowned as she tried to imagine a life with a man so opposed to compromise on something that basic. "It'd be hard on kids, too."

"Yeah," Grady said meeting her eyes, "it would be." He inclined his head slightly to the side and smiled. "I've seen it work, though."

Jenna found herself gliding closer to him as their voices dropped. "Does that mean you've changed your mind about having a family?" she asked.

Grady was suddenly very still. "According to you, I already have one."

Jenna's temper kicked into full gear. She wasn't used to having her word questioned. "Having a son isn't the same as having a wife and child," Jenna retorted, working to keep her voice as serene as she knew she appeared.

"Tell me about it," he drawled.

Jenna flushed self-consciously. Without warning, she had an idea what it would be like to be Grady's wife, to wake up with him every morning, to lie in his arms every night. The thought was as tantalizing as it was disturbing. Being near him was like playing near a fire. Too far away, she'd never get warm. Too close to the flame and she'd get burned. Deciding it was best to just keep a fair distance from him, she planted her hands on her hips and told him, "You cannot just run over me like a steamroller."

"I never said I wanted to."

Maybe not, but right now he looked like he wanted her in his bed again, Jenna realized with equal parts anticipation and anxiety. That was a dangerous proposition, indeed. Grady was the kind of man she could fall in love with. Indeed, part of her felt she had already fallen in love with him. Maybe would always be in love with him a little...

Turning away from Grady, Jenna went to the refrigerator. She took a package of hamburger patties and a bag of fries from the freezer compartment.

"Can I help you there?" He looked over her shoulder as she continued the dinner preparations.

"No. Thanks." Jenna added a package of hamburger buns to the food on the counter.

Grady watched as she took a skillet and a baking sheet from the cabinet. "Then what can I do?"

Jenna set them both on the top of the stove. "Find out who kidnapped Andy, and then get the hell out of my life."

Grady grinned at her unabridged version of her thoughts. "I don't think I can do that," he said as she tore off the cellophane and separated the hamburger patties with a knife.

Jenna removed the paper from the patties and slid them into the skillet. "I don't know why not."

"Oh, yes, Jenna," Grady said softly. Suddenly his hand was on her face, and he was lifting her mouth to his, ducking his head. "I think you do," he said softly, his eyes beginning to close. "I think—"

He was about to kiss her when suddenly he jerked away. Jenna frowned. What the—

Holding on to her with one hand, Grady reached for the marble rolling pin on the counter with the other. Jenna stiffened in his arms as she felt him tense. "What is it?" Her voice was panicked.

His arm sliding around her waist, Grady ducked his head a little lower and whispered in her ear, "There's someone outside your kitchen window."

Panic welled up in Jenna, fierce and unrelenting. "Oh, God," she said, already beginning to tremble.

"Relax," Grady instructed softly, his hand tightening on her spine. He pressed her possessively close as he promised, "I'll handle it."

Jenna's fingers bit into his forearms. Her slender body trembling harder than ever, she tilted her head and looked into his eyes. The feel of his strong, hard body pressed against hers was wildly sensual. And it filled her with an excitement that had nothing to do with the intruder lurking outside. "You're not going to go out there. Are you?" she whispered huskily, the protectiveness she felt for him revealed in the low tremor that was her voice.

Grady grinned broadly. "And I thought you didn't care about me," he murmured sexily, pressing her even closer.

Jenna flushed hotly as his lips tugged on the curve of her ear, sending another frisson of sensation coursing hotly through her veins. "I don't."

Grady's steely blue eyes twinkled. "I'll be the judge of that," he said, and then the laughter left his eyes. He looked like he wanted to make love to her, there, that second. "Kiss me again," he urged roughly. "And make it look really distracting." Giving her no chance to argue, he lowered his mouth to hers. Jenna tasted the sweetness that was Grady, felt his wildness in the plundering, demanding sweep of his tongue. God, she had missed him, she thought as he continued to shower her with hot, passionate kisses and kneaded her back with hungry impatience. She had missed this.

But there was no time for further exploration. Grady lifted his mouth from hers. Gazing into her eyes, with a seriousness that let her know he was simply buying them some time to make some plans for their defense, he demanded, "Were you expecting anyone?"

Oh, God. The intruder. For a second, she'd been so caught up in Grady's kiss, she'd forgotten. Her throat unbearably dry, she shook her head and said, "No—Grady—I—"

Frowning at the edge of panic in her voice, he lowered his head and kissed her again, hard.

Vibrantly aware of the swift state of her own arousal and the way her lower body seemed to automatically mold to his, Jenna struggled to keep her emotions out of the kiss. And found, just as she had predicted, that it was a battle she just couldn't win. She wanted Grady. Always had, and probably always would. It didn't matter that these lust-at-first-sight feelings were quite unlike her. When she was in his arms, all she could think about, all she could do, was surrender. Surrender and make the absolute most of the moment given her.

Reluctantly, Grady broke off their kiss. And wished again she didn't look so damn vulnerable. "Stay calm," Grady ordered against her mouth.

Jenna nodded, letting him know she understood. She knew it was foolhardy of her, but she wished he didn't have to let her go now, just when things were really starting to heat up between them once again.

"And stay here," Grady continued firmly. He leaned forward, pressing another all-for-show kiss into her hair as he whispered his intentions softly in her ear. "I'm going around front to check this out."

The thought of anything happening to him filled Jenna with panic. "Grady, no—" Her hands clutched his shirtfront before he could step away from her. She tilted her head and looked into his ruggedly handsome face. "Let's just call the police," she said.

Grady extricated her fingers from his shirt and lifted them to his mouth. "Hell, Jenna," he said lightly, kissing her knuckles as he shook his head at her in silent remonstration, "I am the police."

The moment Grady was out the door, Jenna grabbed the phone with one hand and began dialing the Hudson Falls sheriff's office in case Grady needed backup. But even before she finished dialing, she heard a shout of alarm. Dropping the phone, she rushed to the window and saw two men tussling in the dark. Several quick moves later, Grady emerged the victor. Jenna went to the phone. She was still dialing as Grady hauled the intruder in.

"You know this clown?" he demanded breathlessly.

Jenna gasped as she got a look at the man's face.

Chapter Seven

"Do you know this guy, Jenna?" Grady growled the moment he had shoved their intruder in the kitchen door.

"Know me!" the burly man with the wavy black hair croaked as indignantly as he could, considering Grady had both his arms pinned behind his back and a nice, subduing choke hold around his neck. "She was married to me!"

Grady loosened his grip on the man's throat. Now that he took a closer look at the guy in the light, he could see he had a patrician look about him. His black hair was shot through with gray. Ditto his thick mustache. His pin-striped wool suit, starched dove gray shirt and coordinating tie indicated he was a professional person, and judging from the quality of the cloth, a highly successful one, at that. Grady loosened his grip a little more and took a wild guess. "Baxter?"

His captive stiffened. "I see you've heard about me."

"And then some." Grady thought about releasing Jenna's ex, then decided he liked the guy right where he was. He used the toe of his boot to pull a chair forward.

"Who are you?" Baxter asked.

"Grady Noland."

Baxter surmised quickly, "The detective who spoke to my secretary late today?"

"You got that right," Grady said. Keeping one hand securely on Baxter's collar, Grady propped one booted foot on the seat of the chair. "Jenna says you put her in Pinehaven."

Baxter's bushy eyebrows lowered like twin thunderclouds over his black eyes. "It was for her own good," Baxter asserted grimly.

Grady shot Jenna a look and saw her breathe a sigh of relief. He knew what she was thinking—that finally someone had corroborated her story. Of course it didn't make him feel very good to realize it had been an untrustworthy, peeping Tom of an ex-husband who'd done the corroborating, but beggars couldn't be choosers.

He made a mental note to check with the staff at Pinehaven first thing tomorrow, and to check with the New York state health department about Pinehaven directly after that. He wanted to know what kind of reputation that place had.

Figuring he had sufficiently intimidated the pediatric surgeon, Grady removed his boot from the chair and shoved Baxter into the chair. Grady leaned over him. Calling on his years of experience in police interrogations, he leaned over Baxter and said calmly, "Second question. What were you doing snooping in the bushes?"

Baxter looked at him. Whatever thoughts he'd had about not cooperating with Grady, and Grady could tell he'd had some, vanished as he looked into Grady's eyes. Baxter swallowed hard, and his mustache quivered just a bit, but it was Jenna Baxter looked at as he answered, not Grady. "I just found out from Lamar that Jenna had checked herself out of the hospital," he said quietly. "I was worried about her."

Grady cut Jenna a glance, too. If she'd had any feelings for Baxter, he noted with something very closely akin to relief, they weren't showing now. In fact, she looked every bit as irritated as Grady to find Baxter had been snooping outside her house. "Why?" Grady asked, moving slightly to the left so that he stood between Jenna and her ex.

Baxter frowned. Grady saw arrogant self-assurance in his expression. "Because she was very sick," Baxter said.

Jenna looked at Grady as if to say I told you so. Grady had never resented a man more than he did at that moment. He wanted to throttle Baxter for having Jenna put away against her will, even for a brief time. And he could tell, just by looking at him, that Baxter was exactly the kind of guy who would do such a despicable thing.

"The only sicko around here is you, Baxter," Grady growled.

"I don't have to listen to this." Baxter started to stand.

Grady shoved him back in the seat, hard. Hands flat on the table, he leaned over him. "How long have you been spying on your ex-wife?"

"This is the first time."

"Yeah, right." Grady looked at Jenna. "I say you should have him arrested."

"What the hell for?" Baxter asked, and then flushed a bright red.

Grady straightened slowly, knowing he'd just driven home his point. "Trespassing, for starters," Grady said.

"Jenna—" Baxter looked at her imploringly. "What's going on here? Who is this?"

"This, Baxter, is my baby's father."

Baxter looked shell-shocked. Grady felt a little stunned, too. He hadn't expected Jenna to admit to it so bluntly when she'd gone to so much trouble earlier to keep her one brief fling with him secret.

Baxter's skin began to look even more mottled. "That again? Jenna, I thought we'd covered that particular delusion. If you want a baby of your own, I'd be happy to—" Baxter frowned as an infant's wail sounded in the distance. He blinked. And blinked again. "What was that?"

"My delusion," Jenna said dryly. "If you gentlemen will excuse me, I have maternal duties to attend to.'' Leaving Baxter with Grady, she slipped from the room. Grady saw Baxter was about to follow her and clamped a firm hand on Baxter's shoulder. ''The truth. Did you have anything to do with the kidnapping?''

''No,'' Baxter said, as Jenna came into the room, a gurgling Andy in her arms. ''Cross my heart. I didn't. I didn't even know there was a baby.''

Grady studied Baxter's face. If Jenna's ex was lying, he was a hell of an actor, because the guy looked absolutely stunned.

''Well, there was a baby,'' Jenna retorted shortly.

''But how—'' Baxter said.

''The usual way,'' Grady said, staking his claim.

Baxter turned even redder. Jenna glared at Grady. ''It's a long story,'' she said. ''One I have no intention of going into.''

Baxter's glance went from Jenna to Grady and back again. ''My God,'' he whispered. ''The two of you really—''

''Yes, Baxter, we did,'' Jenna said dryly. ''But that isn't an issue here right now. What's done is done. I've felt that way for a long time.''

''That's why you've been staying out at the farm,'' Baxter mumbled, still in shock. ''That's why you've been running the foundation from here!''

''Yes,'' Jenna said. She went to the refrigerator and removed a bottle of formula. She carried it to the microwave, slid it inside and punched the defrost button. ''I wanted to keep my pregnancy secret.''

"Well, you did that, all right," Baxter mused. He shook his head. "And I thought... The nursery... Oh, my God, Jenna! I'm sorry."

Suddenly it all made sense. "You took the furniture, didn't you?" Jenna asked gently.

Baxter nodded, watching as Jenna strapped Andy into the baby seat on the counter. "I came out here a couple days after you were put in Pinehaven, not sure what I was going to find. When I saw all the baby furniture... I knew we hadn't been together and you weren't the type to—" Baxter paused and threw an accusing glance at Grady "—sleep around, so I just figured...well, I just thought it was a sign of how sick you were. I had all the furniture put in storage so you wouldn't have to deal with it when you came home from the hospital."

Jenna took the bottle from the microwave, shook it vigorously, then tested it on the inside of her wrist. "You didn't tell my father what you'd found?"

"I didn't want to worry Lamar. He was already just sick about the way you seemed to have fallen apart."

Jenna sighed. Shaking her head in mute dismay, she unstrapped Andy, picked him up and began giving him his bottle.

Deciding finally that Baxter was an idiot but no threat, Grady stepped back. Baxter got up. "I'm sorry, Jenna." He crossed to her side.

"I want Andy's things back," Jenna said. To Grady's surprise, she didn't seem angry. Just resigned. Accepting. He wondered at her ability to forgive the guy so easily. In her place, Grady knew hell would have frozen over before he'd had a kind word to say to the guy.

"I have surgery tomorrow morning, but I'll make arrangements to have someone bring the baby's things back first thing," Baxter promised. He studied his ex-wife. Grady could see the guy still cared about Jenna a lot. And though he didn't like Baxter's continuing affection for his ex, he understood it. Jenna would be a hard woman to let go.

"You really are okay?" Baxter asked Jenna gently.

Jenna released a tremulous sigh. "I will be," she announced, "as soon as I figure out who kidnapped Andy."

Baxter looked at Grady accusingly. "Are you sure it's not him?" Baxter asked Jenna suspiciously.

Jenna rolled her eyes. Deciding Andy had had enough, she put him up on her shoulder and patted him on the back. "Grady didn't know about the baby, either, Baxter," Jenna said.

"That must mean you're not very involved with him," Baxter guessed triumphantly.

The hell she's not, Grady thought, but figuring that sentiment could best be expressed later, in private, Grady kept his counsel.

"I love you, Jenna," Baxter said softly. "I never stopped. I know we had a lot of problems—"

Now Grady felt like a peeping Tom.

"Baxter, please," Jenna said wearily. When Andy burped, she put him down in her arms and began feeding him his bottle again. "We've been over this."

"We've talked about how you feel," Baxter corrected. "Not how I feel. And I'm still in love with you, Jenna. I always will be."

Grady had had enough of *The Young and the Stupid* for one day. "Okay, time to go." Grady grabbed Baxter by the arm and shoved him toward the door.

"Jenna, don't let him do this," Baxter said, casting her a beseeching look over his shoulder.

"He's right," Jenna said. "It is time for you to go."

"You're not going to respond to what I told you?" Baxter asked incredulously.

Jenna sighed. "Baxter, your wanting me to love you doesn't make it so."

Baxter's face tightened into a mask of displeasure. "We're not through here, Jenna," he said. He stormed out.

Grady followed him.

When he came inside minutes later and set the alarm, Jenna was not in the kitchen. He followed the sounds of soft, feminine, slightly off-key singing and found Jenna in the living room. She was seated in the rocking chair, Andy on her lap.

"He's gone," Grady said.

Jenna nodded but said nothing in response. Grady thought she had never looked more beautiful than she did at that moment, with her hair all loose and flowing, her baby, their baby, cradled lovingly in her arms.

He wanted to go to her and take her and the baby in his arms and tell them both he was sorry he hadn't been there for Andy's birth. He wanted to cuddle Andy for a while, and then put the baby to bed, and take Jenna to bed. But none of that was about to happen tonight, Grady realized grimly, reading the hands-off body language Jenna was giving out.

He strolled into the room and took a seat on the end of the sofa. He figured if she had a gripe, she might as well voice it. "You're angry with me, aren't you?"

Again, Jenna shrugged and said nothing.

Frustrated that she was not talkative for once in her life, Grady clasped his hands loosely between his spread thighs and leaned closer. "Look, so I was a little rough with your ex," he began conversationally. "He deserved it for hiding in your bushes and scaring you half to death."

"It's not that," Jenna said softly. She smiled at Andy, who was gazing at her adoringly with his big, baby blue eyes. She continued to rock back and forth serenely.

Grady waited. When no other explanation was forthcoming, he said, "Then what is it?"

Jenna lifted her head. Her dark green eyes lasered into his. "It's the way you acted when he was here."

Grady felt the impact of her steady gaze like the punishing lash of a whip. He didn't know why, but suddenly he was in deep trouble here. "What do you mean?"

Jenna arched a slender brow. "Proprietary. Like you *owned* me or something."

Now that she mentioned it, that was the way he had acted. It was also the way he felt. Now that he knew the baby was in all probability his and Jenna's baby, Grady had a lot at stake. It annoyed him to find that Jenna wasn't more grateful to have him close by, to save her from jerks like Baxter. His mouth tightened as he felt his grip on his temper loosen, but he kept his voice calm. "I was protecting you."

In the soft light of the living room, her classically beautiful features—the high, jutting cheekbones, the deep-set eyes, the feminine line of her jaw—were more pronounced. As was her displeasure with him. "Did it ever occur to you I don't need protecting?" she said.

"The events of the last couple of weeks say otherwise," Grady disagreed.

Jenna glared at him, stood and handed him his son. "Here," she said tightly. "You can rock Andy to sleep." She marched to the door, her full skirt swirling enticingly around her knees.

Grady followed her to the coatrack. "Where are you going?" he demanded.

Jenna shrugged on her coat and lifted the hair away from her neck. It spilled across her collar in glorious strawberry blond waves. "Out."

Grady shifted the warm bundle in his arms a little higher. He didn't like feeling like a jealous spouse, but that was exactly what he felt like. "At this time of night?" He regarded her with disapproval.

Jenna shrugged and refused to meet his eyes. "I've got some things to work out," she said evasively.

Grady had the sudden impression he wasn't just being held at arm's length, but pushed away. For good. The thought was damn disturbing, particularly since he hadn't figured he'd ever want to be fenced in by marriage or any other relationship-style commitment again. And yet here he was, wanting Jenna back in his bed, and in his life, for good. What kind of spell had she put on him? And what did it matter anyway, as long as it lasted? "Jenna—" His voice was soft, conciliatory.

Her reaction was not. Her fists clenched in front of her, she spun toward him in a drift of lavender perfume. "If I stay here, Grady, I'm going to explode."

Grady knew how he'd like an argument like this to end—in bed. But he couldn't engineer a solution like that for several reasons, a wide-awake Baby Andy being the least of them. When they were together again, and he was more sure than ever that they would be together again one day soon, he wanted it to be because she wanted to be with him. Because she couldn't live without him. Or at least didn't want to. "I don't like this," he said, hoping his displeasure would have some effect on her.

Again, she disappointed him. "Tough." She sent him a beleaguered smile that mirrored the turbulent emotion in her eyes. "Life is full of things we don't like, Grady Noland. Ask me. I'm an authority on that!"

JENNA DUG HER HANDS in her pockets and walked the inside fence along the property line. She had been right. The cold air and solitude had been exactly what she needed.

It had been an upsetting few days. An upsetting couple of weeks. Hell, an upsetting year. But having her very own baby to hold and love had made all the heartache worthwhile. If only things had stayed that simple. If only she had been able to go through with the "adoption" of Andy as she had planned, then everything would have been all right. But that hadn't happened, and right now things weren't all right. She still hadn't discovered who had kidnapped Andy or why. Worse, Grady now knew about his son and was behaving possessive.

Maybe that wouldn't have been so bad had Grady believed her story from the very first, but he hadn't. She had bared her soul to him, kissed him like she meant it, trusted him enough to ask him to help her find the kidnapper, and all for what? Grady had listened to her dutifully but he still had plenty of doubts about her. So the bottom line was he still didn't trust her. Never had. Probably never would. Just like Baxter hadn't trusted her when they'd been married. She couldn't live like that again. She just couldn't.

The only thing to do was go back to her original plan and stick to it. She would adopt Andy and continue on as a single mother, Grady or no Grady.

JENNA DIDN'T COME BACK for almost an hour. When she did, her cheeks were flushed with the cold. Her eyes were no less fiery, but she seemed less physically tense than when she had left. And yet there was something different about her, Grady couldn't help but note. Something aloof. It was as if she'd made up her mind about them, and there was no them. Not any longer.

She inhaled the scent of broiled meat and piping hot fries. "You've been cooking."

He nodded. "We didn't get around to eating earlier. I figured you must be famished." Grady motioned to the fax machine in her office. "You had several messages come in while you were gone. One from Switzerland, another from Ethiopia, one from Panama."

She slipped off her coat and walked over to her fax machine. Grady followed her. "Where did you go?"

Jenna glanced up from the fax she was reading, her green eyes deliberately expressionless. Grady had never seen that particular look in her eyes before. He wasn't sure he liked it.

"Is this an inquisition?" she asked.

Grady knew he was supposed to say no. "Maybe," he said.

Their glances held for another long moment. She passed on the opportunity to answer his question and returned to her reading. "Where's Andy?"

"In his crib upstairs. I figured it was time to put him down for the night."

Jenna finished reading her faxes and put them on her desk. "Time for us all to be down for the night," she said. "But dinner first. Did you already eat?"

"I thought I'd wait for you," Grady said.

Jenna looked like she had just found out she hadn't won the lottery, but she made no comment. He followed her down the hall past the stairs to the kitchen. Although he was careful to give her the correct amount of physical space, he couldn't help but track the provocative sway of her hips beneath the swirling wool skirt. With every graceful, feminine step she took, he felt the desire coil more tightly inside him. The depth of possessiveness he was feeling toward Jenna was new to him. He wasn't sure he liked it. "I think you should stay away from Baxter," he said.

Jenna looked as if she had been expecting that. She shook her head in silent bemusement, then sashayed to the refrigerator to get herself a bottle of light beer. "Why?" she quipped as she set her drink on the table, then followed it with mustard, pickles, mayonnaise, catsup, lettuce, tomatoes, onions and cheese. "This may come as news to you, Grady, but it's not up to you to decide whom I see or don't see."

But it was up to him to protect Jenna, Grady thought, whether she wanted him to or not. "Baxter's still in love with you."

Jenna shut the refrigerator with her hip. "So he said," she replied mildly.

"You're not concerned?"

Jenna shrugged. "Having an ex who won't let go seems to be a problem we share," she said, spearing Grady with a laser look. "Besides, with Baxter, it's a matter of ego more than anything else. He's had women falling over him for so long he can't believe that someone might actually not want to be with him."

Grady frowned. Jenna's blasé attitude disturbed him. He removed the plates warming in the oven and carried them to the table. "As far as I'm concerned, he's still a suspect in the kidnapping," Grady continued.

Jenna regarded Grady cautiously. Her conflicting feelings on the subject were reflected in her dark green eyes. "Baxter just told us he didn't do it."

Grady watched her pull up a chair. He got out a beer for himself, twisted off the cap and sat down beside her. "People lie, Jenna, sometimes very convincingly."

Jenna was silent a moment, thinking. Finally, she shook her head. "I know how it looks, but...I have to trust my gut feeling. You're off the mark here, Grady."

Grady paused, perplexed, wanting nothing more at that moment than to take her in his arms. "Why are you defending him when he's already proved himself to be a threat to you and our baby?"

"Our baby?" Jenna interrupted. "You just said our baby, Grady!"

Grady felt the blood move into his face. Jenna was right—he had. It wasn't like him to consider anything a fact before it was a fact. That went contrary to everything he had ever learned in the course of his police work. He had better watch his step here. Clearly, his feelings for Jenna were getting in the way of his deductive reasoning.

"You're getting off the subject, Jenna," Grady reprimanded sternly. "The man convinced your father to put you in a mental hospital."

"He did what he did regarding Pinehaven and the baby furniture because he thought I'd gone off the deep end and he was trying to help, as best he knew how. I don't know who kidnapped my baby, but as soon as I saw Baxter's stunned reaction to Andy tonight, I knew it certainly wasn't Baxter," Jenna said firmly. "And the more I think about it, the more I know I'm right. Baxter just would not hurt me that way.

"Clarissa, on the other hand, is another matter," Jenna continued, picking up steam. "Clarissa not only has a motive for kidnapping Andy, she's manipulative and devious enough to try to carry it off. I think if we have a suspect here, Grady, it's Clarissa, and nothing you can say or do is going to convince me otherwise."

Grady sat back, his arms folded across his chest. "Just so you know, Jenna," he said softly, "I'm checking out Clarissa's documents, too. I faxed copies to my partner while you were out on your walk."

"Oh." Jenna flushed and fell silent. "Does that mean you believe me when I say Andy is our baby?" she asked softly, her jade eyes shining with new hope.

Grady wanted to tell Jenna yes and put her mind at ease, but he couldn't, not without going against every bit of training and experience he'd ever had. "It means," Grady warned cautiously, and watched the hope leave her eyes as suddenly as it had filtered in, "that I'm taking nothing at face value." He knew what he hoped for—that Andy was his baby and Jenna's. But he couldn't, wouldn't, let himself count on that prematurely. "I'll know what the truth is only after all the facts are in."

Chapter Eight

"Do you have any idea what time it is?"

Jenna glanced up at the sound of the low, husky voice. Grady stood framed in the doorway of her office. He was dressed in a pair of jeans and the light blue oxford cloth shirt he'd had on the day before. His mane of shaggy brown hair was mussed from sleep, and his ruggedly handsome face was lined with a day's growth of golden brown beard. He looked like he had just tumbled out of bed, and wanted nothing more than to tumble right back into it again—with her this time. Jenna's heart skipped a beat at the realization of how much Grady still desired her.

But his desiring her again didn't mean he would have her, she thought. Getting involved with Grady would be dangerous, too dangerous for her blood. And she didn't want to be hurt again, not by Grady, not by anyone. "It's three in the morning," Jenna replied. "Go back to bed, Grady."

Grady unfolded his lanky frame from the doorway and stalked closer, his sock-clad feet moving soundlessly on the plushly carpeted floor. He lifted a stack of files from the corner of her desk and sat down. Both feet flat on the floor, his long legs slanting in front of him, he folded his arms across his chest and probed her face with a relentlessly searching glance. "Not until you tell me what you're doing up."

She reached for the telephone receiver and said matter-of-factly, "I'm making some phone calls to Switzerland."

Grady's hand covered hers before she could so much as lift the receiver off its cradle. "Couldn't you do that in the morning?"

Her pulse racing at his nearness, Jenna withdrew her hand from the warmth of his. "I won't be here in the morning." Needing suddenly to put some distance between herself and Grady, she stood and stalked to the file cabinet. She yanked open the drawer, then paused as she saw the red satin heart-shaped box inside.

"What is it?" Grady said, already sliding his hips off her desk.

"Nothing." Tired of Grady nosing into every aspect of her life while granting her no more trust than he would the suspect in one of his cases, Jenna shut the drawer. She was pretty sure, from the handwriting on the envelope and the placement of the gift, that she knew who the present was from, but she would wait to open it in private.

"Nothing, my foot." He stalked past her.

She caught his arm, delaying him. "My files are none of your business."

Grady continued moving, but made no effort to disengage her fingers from his arm. "Until we figure out who kidnapped our baby, Jenna, everything around here is my business."

Determined to hold at least part of her life sacred from his relentless prying, Jenna dropped her hold on his arm and scrambled to stand in front of him. He merely smiled, reached behind her and pulled open the drawer. He frowned at the Valentine's Day candy box and unopened greeting card.

"Baxter," Grady supposed grimly.

"Baxter or no, it's none of your business!" Jenna announced defiantly. Trapped between the half-open file drawer and Grady's tall, lanky body, she was incredibly aware of him, throbbing all over.

"I beg to differ, babe. We're rounding up suspects here. Whoever sent that gift might be one of them." Leaning in closer, he pulled both items from the drawer. Their chests were so close they touched. Jenna felt another tingle of desire move through her.

"It's not from Baxter," Jenna said. She crossed her arms. "Satisfied?"

"No. If it's not from Baxter, then who is it from?" Grady asked as he lifted both items over her head.

Jenna remained stubbornly silent. Looking just as displeased with her as she felt with him, he held the card out to her. "Open it."

Jenna glared at him. Grady was way off base, but it wouldn't do any good to tell him so. "This is how it started with Baxter, too, Grady. Little demands that soon escalated into larger ones. I am not falling into the trap of having a man control my life again, so when I feel like opening it, I will, and not one instant before then.''

Grady's sensual lips thinned authoritatively. He wasn't used to having his orders disregarded and he was fast losing patience with her. ''Last chance, Jenna.''

Jenna mocked him with a look. ''No, this is your last chance. You're dreaming if you think I'm going to let you order me around in my own office!''

He shrugged, not the least bit perturbed by her lack of cooperation. ''Fine, have it your way. Then I'll open the card.'' He started to tear the seal.

Jenna grabbed the card from his hands. ''Like hell you will! It's my card!''

He merely quirked a brow, letting her know with just a look that he'd already made up his mind, too, and if it came down to a physical struggle he'd win.

She held the card to her chest. Her fingers were trembling. She really did not want to get into a physical tussle with Grady, nor did she want to set a precedent with Grady like she had with Baxter by just giving in. Irritated because Grady could make her so edgy and angry all at once, Jenna lifted her chin. ''I'll open it when I want to, and I don't want to right now.''

Grady backed her up. The edge of Jenna's desk collided with her hips. He leaned in. Jenna leaned back, but could go nowhere. She found herself bent backward over her desk. His legs were suddenly pressed against hers. Jenna had to put a hand out behind her to steady herself and keep from falling.

Grady tossed the candy aside, put a palm on either side of her and braced his weight against the top of her desk. His slate-blue eyes roved her upturned face, dropped lower, to linger at the open vee of her satin pajamas. "What are you hiding, Jenna?"

Jenna clutched the unopened card to her chest. The hand she'd put behind her was beginning to tremble with the strain of holding her weight in such an awkward position. "My private life."

Grady's sable brow quirked again. His eyes radiated interest, but no pleasure. "Meaning what? You have another beau?"

Jenna raised a threatening knee to the inside of his thigh. He stepped back defensively. She straightened quickly and did an about-face. Grabbing both card and candy, she sat down, laid them both across her lap, scooted her chair forward until her legs were completely beneath the desk. Her back to Grady, she began typing once again.

She half expected another tussle. Grady merely watched her get comfortable, then sauntered across the room. He stretched out on the sofa with lazy disregard for her presence. As he wedged a throw pillow beneath his head, his shirt fell open even more, revealing more of his sinewy chest with the golden skin and whorls of golden brown hair. Jenna recalled with disturbing clarity how it had felt to run her hands over the solidness of that chest, how it had felt to cuddle against him and wantonly string kisses from throat to navel to...

Damn. She was never going to get any work done with him here, and she had a ton of work to do. She stopped typing but didn't turn to face him. Instead, she continued to regard him out of her peripheral vision. "Now what are you doing?" she demanded tensely.

Grady smiled at her and got even more comfortable in the deep cushions of the floral sofa. "Waiting for you to finish your letter." He turned slightly on his side and propped his head on his hand. "Then we're going to wrestle for that card."

Jenna's pulse points pounded at the heat she heard in his voice. "We are not."

He grinned at her and continued to regard her like a predator stalking his prey. "Wanna bet?"

Jenna released a pent-up breath. She swiveled her chair around so that she was facing Grady directly. "You know I divorced Baxter for this very reason. He was too controlling."

"Lucky for me we're not married then, isn't it?" Grady bounded up from the sofa and closed the distance between them with surprising swiftness. Clamping his hands on the chair arms on either side of her, he leaned down so their faces were almost touching. "Open the card, Jenna," he said softly.

Jenna wished he didn't smell so damn good, like sleep and bedclothes and warm winter nights. She wished she wasn't so familiar with the scent of his spice and sandalwood cologne, or the slightly rougher, very male texture of his skin.

"Come on, Jenna," Grady continued to provoke. He pressed a string of kisses across the crown of her head.

Jenna held herself perfectly still. She knew what he wanted. He wanted her to fight him off so he would have an excuse to tussle with her, but she wasn't going to give it to him, just like she wasn't going to open that card.

"Forget me opening the card, Grady," she said flatly.

"Why?"

Because if I do, I'll have let you seduce me into doing what you want. And that was just as bad, in her mind, as being bullied or coerced into something she didn't want to do.

"Okay." Grady moved away from her with a suddenness that surprised her. He bounded behind her swivel chair toward the phone. "I'll call your father and ask him who the candy might be from. And if he doesn't know, I'll ask Baxter. And if he doesn't know—"

Jenna stayed where she was, knowing he expected her to back down any moment. "Then what?" she taunted, lounging in her chair.

Grady leveled his eyes on hers and kept them there, letting her know in a heartbeat that his determination to get at the truth was every bit as unshakable as hers was to hide it. "Then I'll take out an announcement in the *Times,*" he said softly. Unrepentantly.

Despite her resolve not to show any emotion save bravado, Jenna felt her lips thin into a line of absolute resentment. She had to decide whether to cut her losses and give in or carry this through to the bitter end.

She stared into his eyes that had never seemed so blue to her. She supposed it was the blue in his shirt bringing out the blue in his eyes. Either that, or the subdued light in the study. But the color of his eyes and her attraction to him were neither here nor there, she thought, as she released a beleaguered sigh. Getting caught up on her work was crucial, and she would never get caught up while Grady dogged her about something that had absolutely nothing whatsoever to do with the kidnapping he was investigating.

"You're going to feel awfully silly for being so suspicious when you see who this is from," Jenna predicted as she tore open the card.

Grady looked at the signature inside, then looked again. "Nanny Beth?" he read incredulously. "Why would your nanny give you a Valentine heart full of candy?"

Jenna reached for the candy heart and tore open the seal. "Just to be sweet. She knew it had been a rough year for me." Jenna popped a chocolate in her mouth. It had a gooey caramel center. She handed the box to Grady. He selected one, too.

"Because you were a single mother?" Grady asked.

"And because I felt I had to hide out," Jenna said. In retrospect, she saw that she had been wrong about that, that with time she probably could have gotten her father to understand her decision, if not actually support her in it. But at the time she hadn't wanted to take the risk that her father would track Grady down with a shotgun and try to make him do the decent thing. But someone had, anyway, she thought. And they were no closer to discovering who had taken Andy from his crib.

"It never occurred to you to go back with Baxter?" Grady asked. "He probably would have remarried you, you know, despite the pregnancy."

"Probably," Jenna agreed. She lifted a cup of coffee to her lips. It was ironic. She and Grady had made a child together, but they still knew so little about one another's pasts. Maybe it was time that changed, she thought. Maybe if he knew more about her, maybe he would know she was telling him the truth, and nothing but the truth. Certainly, if he was less suspicious of her, the next few days would be easier on them all.

She searched through the box and found one that looked like a chocolate-covered almond. "But I didn't want that."

Grady helped himself to more candy, too. He studied her. "Why not?"

"Because our marriage had already failed once," Jenna explained.

"What went wrong?" Grady moved to the small sideboard in the corner and helped himself to some of the coffee Jenna had fixed earlier.

"In a word, everything," Jenna replied as she got up to get another cup of coffee.

Grady waited until she had finished pouring her coffee, then tangled his fingers with hers and led her over to the sofa. He sat in one corner. Jenna sat in the other. "How did the two of you meet?" he asked.

Jenna lifted her coffee cup to her lips and took a sip. "We met through my work for the Children's Rescue Foundation. He volunteered his services for some needy children in South America. I was there during the month he did the surgeries. I saw what a dramatic difference his skills made in those children's lives, and I fell a little in love with that. We had a whirlwind courtship and married as soon as we got back to the States. And it was then that things began to go sour between us."

Grady downed half his coffee in a single gulp, then rested his cup on his thigh. "Sour how?" Grady asked gently.

"Baxter expected me to be a figurehead boss, not a real one, at the Foundation. When I refused to devote all my time to being a doctor's wife, he became very suspicious. He accused me of not wanting to stop working because I was secretly having flings with doctors and lawyers and professionals I met around the world in the course of my work. I figured that he would relax as time went on when he saw this truly was not the case. So I tried never to chide him when he called me in the middle of the night, or popped up unexpectedly to surprise me when I was on a business trip, or embarrassed me in front of family or friends or staff with some of his detective-style questions. But when a whole year passed and he was still as suspicious and controlling as ever, I knew that he wasn't ever going to change. I couldn't live that way, knowing my own husband didn't trust me. And I also knew,'' Jenna continued sadly, ''that I wasn't in love with him and I never had been. I had only been in love with what he'd done for the children. Despite everything, Baxter is a selfless humanitarian and a wonderful physician. So I asked him for a divorce.''

Grady finished the rest of his coffee in a single draft. ''How'd he take it?''

''He was angry at first—but then he just kind of dug in where he was. You know, maintained his ties with my family. Kissed up to my dad and all that.''

Grady got up to get himself another cup of coffee. When he returned, he didn't sit in the opposite corner of the sofa, but in the middle. ''And your dad bought it?''

Jenna pulled her bent knee in toward her body, so it would no longer be touching Grady's thigh. ''My dad wanted me to be married and have a family. He knew Baxter was a good man.''

Jenna went to the coffeemaker. She thought about having another cup, but decided she was too wired already. She turned the coffeemaker off, put her cup aside, and because it was the only other truly comfortable place in the office to sit and still have a quiet conversation with him, she went to join Grady on the sofa once again.

Grady waited until she had curled up in her own corner of the sofa cross-legged. "Did your father know you weren't in love with Baxter?"

She frowned as she traced a mindless pattern on her bare ankle. "My father has always felt I was far too picky when it came to men."

Grady's eyes followed her index finger as it strayed to the tip of her ballerina slipper and slipped idly beneath the edge. "Picky how?" he persisted.

"I just want the guy I'm with to be perfect."

"And if he's not?"

She looked up at Grady and offered him a deadpan grin. "Then I lose interest."

"Maybe you just haven't loved the right guy," he teased, but there was an underlying seriousness to his twinkling gaze that suddenly had her senses in an uproar.

Jenna struggled to retain control of her soaring emotions. "And who would the right guy be, Grady?" she shot back facetiously, aware her heart was pounding again in a way that had nothing to do with the caffeine she had just consumed. "You, I suppose?"

"Maybe," Grady allowed, still holding her gaze.

Jenna drew a shaky breath. It was time to end this intimate little early-morning tête-à-tête. It was a tête-à-tête like this that had gotten her into trouble in the first place, she thought.

She bounded up from the sofa. "Maybe not."

Grady bounded up right after her. He caught her arm and pulled her gently around to face him so they were standing toe-to-toe, face-to-face. "I'm sorry you had to spend Valentine's Day the way you did," he said softly, meaning it.

Jenna suddenly found she had to swallow or not breathe. She drew a shaky breath. "I got over it," she said.

"Yeah, I know," Grady drawled. "The question is, will you get over this?" He lowered his head and delivered a gentle kiss. "Will either of us, Jenna?"

He kissed her again. Her lips parted beneath the pressure of his as his tongue swept her mouth in long, sensuous strokes. His hands circled her tightly and pressed her more fully into his arms until Jenna's whole body was alive, quivering with urgent sensations unlike any she had ever felt. She moaned and allowed him to press her closer. The satin of her pajama top was little protection against the hardness of his chest. Her nipples beaded and ached as he crushed her closer. Her abdomen felt liquid and weightless, her knees weak. And where he pressed against her so intimately, hardness to softness, there was a tingling ache. It had been so long, she thought. Too long.

Jenna wanted so badly to give in to him, to the desire seductively inundating them both. But even as he kissed her again, dipping his tongue into her mouth with practiced, honeyed strokes, she knew she couldn't give in and still keep her wits about her. And for Andy's sake, for her own, she needed to maintain her ability to think straight, to reason, to act like a responsible adult, not a lovestruck teen.

Her mind made up, she planted a hand firmly on his chest and pushed. Grady lifted his mouth immediately—well, almost immediately, she thought as her lips continued to burn and tingle and crave even more of his plundering kisses. She stepped back, aware she wasn't the only one trembling like a leaf in the wind this time. So, she thought with distinctly feminine if somewhat irrational satisfaction, Grady was having trouble dealing with his feelings, too. Good. She hoped he ached all night, because she was certainly going to!

"You insist on pushing the limits, don't you?" she asserted angrily, all too aware how close she had come to going to bed with him again. One more kiss, one touch of his hand to her breast, and she would have been his...maybe not for all time, but for tonight. Jenna groaned. It was all she could do to keep from burying her face in her hands. When would she ever learn?

Grady wrapped a lock of her hair around his fingertip. "Pushing limits is my specialty," he teased without one iota of remorse.

As if I didn't know, Jenna thought morosely. Grady's bad-boy sensuality was a big part of what had attracted her to him in the first place, that and the compassion and tenderness she saw in his eyes. But bad boys who didn't believe in marriage did not make good fathers, she told herself sternly, and Andy needed a father. "I'm not getting involved with you again," Jenna insisted flatly, meaning every word more than ever.

Grady merely looked at her. "We'll see."

"HEY, JENNA, is this an okay time?" Steve Jackson asked as he handed her the morning paper.

"It's fine." Jenna greeted her father's young assistant warmly. At age twenty-six, he was several years younger than her. Lamar had hired the MBA grad straight out of Penn's prestigious Wharton School of Business, and Jenna knew it had been one of the smartest things her father had ever done. Steve was nice and easygoing, with a decidedly optimistic outlook on life and a can-do attitude Lamar appreciated. Steve never complained about having to work overtime. No chore was too big or too small for him. On the few occasions Jenna had visited the corporate offices to see her father, she had enjoyed hanging out with Steve precisely because he was so easy to get along with. "What brings you all the way out here?" she continued.

"Your dad wanted me to check up on you before I went to work this morning, to make sure you were all right and everything."

"Well, as you can see, I'm fine," Jenna said.

Steve turned as an Acme Furniture Storage truck pulled into the drive behind his black Porsche. "You expecting them?"

Jenna frowned thoughtfully. "Baxter said he'd return Andy's baby furniture today."

Steve whistled long and low. "Yeah, I know. He sure didn't waste any time, did he?"

Jenna ushered Steve inside. She took his navy trench coat and hung it on the coatrack, then led him to the kitchen and poured him a cup of coffee. "How did you know about that?"

Steve bent in front of the baby swing and tickled Andy under the chin. "Baxter came to see your dad last night."

"Before or after he'd seen me?" Jenna asked.

"After. Anyway, I happened to be there. Your dad and I had been working on the advertising budget for the rest of the year. So I heard part of the story," Steve said. Straightening, he helped himself to a Danish and took a big bite. "I have to tell you, Lamar was pretty hot about Baxter breaking in here and putting all your baby furniture in storage without telling anyone what he'd done. He read Baxter the riot act for interfering that way."

Aware the baby swing was running out of steam, Jenna gave it another crank and a little push. Andy smiled and cooed with delight as the swing picked up speed. "How did Baxter take it?" Jenna asked, hoping there hadn't been a fight. She didn't need any more stress in her life right now.

"Well, surprisingly enough, Baxter agreed completely with your dad. He said he realized when he saw you and the baby last night that he had overstepped his bounds."

Which is why he's making good on his promise to have everything moved back so fast, Jenna thought, *because he wants me to know he is serious about making amends.*

"Was that all Baxter said?"

"Well, actually he started to say something about Pinehaven—if that means anything to you—but then Lamar shushed him up and asked me to leave, so I did."

So Steve didn't know she had been in Pinehaven, Jenna thought. Ten to one, no one except Baxter and her father and now Grady did, either. Probably not even her brother, Kip...

The sound of the doorbell brought Jenna out of her thoughts. She returned to the front door, and the delivery men began bringing things in. For the next several minutes Jenna was completely occupied as she directed them where to take the crib and dresser and changing table. Ten minutes later, everything was in place more or less as it had been. Jenna signed for the things and then watched as the van took off. She had just shut the door again when Grady walked down the steps. Just out of the shower, he looked fresh and handsome and vital. He glanced at Steve Jackson, who was coming out of the kitchen with Andy in his arms. "He was a little tired of the swing, and started to fuss, so I picked him up," Steve said. "I hope you don't mind."

Jenna smiled at Steve. "Not at all." Aware Grady was regarding them both with an interested look, Jenna made introductions, finishing with, "Steve just dropped by to check in on me." She looked at Steve, who, with his precision-cut dark brown hair and Armani suit, looked every bit the successful young executive. "I know you just had a Danish, but if you'd like to stay for a proper brunch, I'd be glad to fix you whatever you like," Jenna finished.

Steve flushed with pleasure. "Normally I would take you up on that, but your dad needs me at a meeting with the franchisers at eleven-thirty, so I better hotfoot it back to Albany unless I want to be late. I'll tell him you're looking well, though. And so's the baby."

"Thanks, Steve, I'd appreciate it."

"And Jenna?" Steve paused. "I don't know a lot about what's been going on with you lately. Your dad just said you'd had a baby and were still trying to decide what to do about...well, you know, everything. I just want you to know I'm happy that everything seems to be going so great for you. You're a great gal, and the apple of your dad's eye, but then you know that." Steve hung his head shyly as he ran out of steam.

"Yeah, I guess I do." Jenna smiled, touched by Steve's boyish enthusiasm. She gently touched his arm. "And just so you know, my dad is always talking about how much initiative you have. He says he barely knows there's a problem before you're doing something to fix it. He really thinks you're doing a great job."

"I really try," Steve gushed as he struggled into his trench coat. "Your dad's given me a hell of an opportunity, putting me on the fast track to a vice presidency at Sullivan Shoes. I want to make sure he's getting his money's worth."

"Well, he is." Jenna showed Steve to the door. "Tell my dad when you see him I'll try to stop by to see him just as soon as I can."

"Do you know when that will be?" Steve asked as he paused in the portal. He shot a cautious look at Grady, who was standing by politely, taking in every word.

"Just as soon as I get things wrapped up here," Jenna promised. She said goodbye to Steve.

As soon as she shut the door, she turned to Grady. "That was completely unnecessary, you know."

"What?" Grady feigned innocence.

"The way you just checked out Steve Jackson."

Grady shrugged. "Until we discover who kidnapped Andy everyone who comes in and out of this house is a possible suspect."

Jenna shifted Andy to her other arm. She could tell by the way he leaned his head against her shoulder that he was getting sleepy again. She went up the stairs and into her bedroom and put Andy in the cradle. He settled onto his tummy with nary a whimper. Jenna covered him with a blanket and crept out again.

Andy was still quiet.

She took the baby monitor and went into the bath across the hall. "This is my house, Grady," Jenna said, picking up the argument where it had left off.

Grady followed her into the bath and with a wary glance across the hall shut the door. "And that's my son," he said flatly.

Jenna had been brushing her hair into smooth waves. She paused and put down the brush, feeling a crazy mixture of emotion running riot inside her. "You sound pretty sure about that, all of a sudden," she said.

Grady folded his arms and leaned against the door. "Shouldn't I be?" His eyes met hers. Once again, he was weighing everything she said and did.

Jenna turned to the mirror. "I am not having this discussion," she said.

"Yes, Jenna, we are."

"Right." She clipped the length of her hair in a gold clasp at the nape of her neck, spritzed on some perfume and headed for the door.

Grady continued to block her way. Evidently realizing that ordering her around didn't work, he tried a different tack. "Wait a minute, Jenna—"

"No," Jenna said hotly. She waved a lecturing finger beneath his nose. "You wait a minute. You have no claim on me."

Grady put a hand on her shoulder. "If Andy's my son—" he began calmly.

Jenna removed his hand like an odious scrap of garbage. "So it's *if* now?"

Grady scowled. "You know what I mean."

"Yes, I do, and that's what bothers me," Jenna snapped. Needing to do something, anything, except look into his eyes, she leaned toward the mirror and picked up her lipstick. "If Andy turns out to be your son, then you want to get serious with me," she said, pausing to outline her lips in muted peach. "And if he doesn't, I can just forget it."

Grady looked into the mirror and watched her rub her lips together to set the lipstick. "If he isn't my son, it means you've lied to me."

Her temper soaring, Jenna spun around to face him. "That's not the point."

Grady leaned in closer. "Then what is the point?" he demanded in a tone that was just as fiery.

Jenna stabbed a finger at his chest. "The point is you should already know the truth in your heart, Grady. We should never have had to go for blood tests or wait for results. The point is you should have known the truth the first moment the words came out of my mouth." She shook her head in silent recrimination. "The fact you didn't... Well, I just can't live that way!" Pushing him aside, she was out of the bathroom and down the stairs like a shot.

He followed her to the first floor. "Jenna, I am investigating a kidnapping here."

"So that makes it okay for you not to accept anything I tell you at face value? So that makes it okay for you to make a federal case out of a simple Valentine's Day gift? I can't live this way again, Grady, and damn it, I won't!" Jenna pulled a burgundy wool reefer from the front hall closet.

Grady jammed his hands on his hips. He regarded her with growing impatience. "I'm a cop, Jenna. This is how cops operate."

"And I'm a person, Grady," Jenna retorted, echoing his harsh, pragmatic tone. "A flesh-and-blood person, with feelings!"

He watched her shrug into her coat and stomp to the front door. His lips thinned in irritation. "Where are you going now?"

"Out!" Jenna grabbed her keys and purse.

"To do what?"

My own sleuthing, Jenna thought. Because while she had been working in the office last night, she had known there was someone else they had to investigate. Someone Grady knew nothing about. Someone close to her who might have taken Andy in a misguided effort to help her. "I have to send those papers I typed up last night by overnight mail," she told him, going into the office to pick up the packages she had prepared.

Grady frowned. "Can't you fax them?"

"No."

"Then wait a bit, until Andy wakes up, and I'll go with you," he suggested.

Jenna shook her head firmly. "No, Grady, I need to be alone." She had to figure out how she felt about Grady. She had to figure out why she couldn't seem to stop kissing or wanting or dreaming about him, when he was so clearly wrong for her. Grady stopped arguing abruptly and gave her a hard look. She had the uneasy feeling he knew she wasn't telling him the whole truth, but she couldn't worry about that now.

Chapter Nine

"You look great, Jenna," her brother Kip said the moment he stepped out of the Jetway at the Albany Airport, his beautiful, dark-haired wife at his side. "But what are you doing here? Leslie and I weren't expecting anyone to meet our plane." He paused, his expression turning slightly worried. "Everything's okay, isn't it?"

"Yes and no," Jenna said tensely. Looking at Kip in his Hawaiian duds and winter suntan, a lei still wrapped around his neck, she found it hard to believe that anyone as laid-back and fun-loving as her older brother could be devious enough to kidnap Andy, drop him at Alec's, then just leave on vacation. But Kip and Leslie had been the only ones in her family who knew about Andy's birth. And they had disapproved vigorously of her decision to go it alone, so that made them prime suspects. She just hadn't wanted to face it before, because she had always felt Kip was on her side. Jenna swallowed hard. "Can we talk?"

"Sure." Looking both bewildered and concerned, Kip and Leslie accompanied Jenna over to a deserted corner of the passenger area outside the gate. Jenna noted that Leslie looked just as tanned, happy and relaxed as Kip did. Part of her was very glad about that. She adored Leslie as much as Kip did.

"So how's Andy?" Kip whispered.

"Just fine."

Kip searched her face. "No second thoughts?" he asked.

Plenty, Jenna thought, but not about having the baby, rather getting involved with Grady. So what if the chemistry between them was still as potent as ever? So what if he not only seemed to hit it off with Andy right away, but was feeling downright protective of their baby? He didn't love her. Sure, he might be willing to marry her, for the baby's sake, but she didn't want to be married because Grady felt an obligation to Andy. She wanted Grady to marry her because he was wildly in love with her and couldn't live without her. Anything else just wouldn't do.

"You know, Jenna, our offer is still good," Leslie added. "Kip and I will—" She cast a furtive look over her shoulder to make sure no one was within earshot. "Well, you know..." she whispered.

"Adopt?" Jenna supplied dryly.

"Right," Kip said.

"It's not as if we'd be doing anything we hadn't planned, since Kip and I are already on the waiting lists at several private adoption agencies."

Jenna tucked a lock of her strawberry blond hair behind one ear. "I appreciate what you've offered to do. What I didn't appreciate was the kidnapping."

Kip paled. "What kidnapping?"

Briefly, Jenna explained, watching their faces all the while for the slightest show of culpability. To her frustration, she saw none. They seemed as in the dark about everything as she was.

"Why didn't you call us?" Kip interrupted as Jenna was describing the abduction. "Dammit, Jenna, you know that Leslie and I would have come home immediately!"

Relief flowed through Jenna as she realized she could still trust Kip and his wife, that she hadn't been wrong about them. She shrugged. "I thought about it as soon as I realized Andy wasn't in the house. But then I got to thinking that maybe you two had told Dad about the baby, because you were so worried about me, and that Dad had taken him."

"We told you that your secret was safe with us," Kip said.

"Even if we didn't approve of your decision to keep his birth secret," Leslie added.

"Furthermore, you know me better than that," Kip reminded her sternly. "I don't renege on promises." He paused. "I assume you found Andy... didn't you?"

"A few days ago."

Kip did a double take as that sunk in. "Not until then?" he said incredulously.

Jenna told them about Pinehaven. Kip scowled. "Just like Baxter to muddle things up with his self-centered misdiagnosis of the situation. When is that guy going to realize the two of you aren't still married?"

Soon, if Grady had anything to do with it, Jenna thought. "So you didn't tell Dad or anyone else—anyone at all—about Andy?" Jenna persisted.

"We swore we wouldn't." Kip looked at Leslie.

Leslie looked at Kip. "Not a soul," she said.

"And you had nothing whatsoever to do with the kidnapping," Jenna continued doggedly.

"Nothing at all," Kip and Leslie said in unison.

"Then I don't understand," Jenna said, throwing up her hands in frustration. "Who took Andy from his crib on Valentine's Day? Who left that note?"

Kip and Leslie shook their heads. Obviously, they were as baffled as Jenna was. "I wish I could tell you," Kip said. "But honestly, I haven't a clue."

Jenna looked up and swore.

"What is it?" Kip touched her arm.

Jenna covered her face with her palm. Her whole life was turning into a perfect proof of Murphy's law. "Don't look now, but here comes father and son."

It annoyed her to see how right the two males looked together, like a father and son should. Grady's shaggy, sable brown hair was wind-tossed, his cheeks and nose red with the cold, his blue eyes alert and furious. Yet he carried the two-month-old infant with the tender sensibility of an old pro. And it was clear that Andy, who was bundled up in a powder blue snowsuit and matching knit infant cap, was happy to be with his dad. Wide-awake and flashing delighted smiles at everyone around him, Andy nestled contentedly in the cozy nook formed by Grady's shoulder, chest and arm.

Four long lazy strides later, Grady joined the group. His eyes lasered in on Jenna's. "Get your Federal Express package mailed?" he asked her mildly.

Ignoring his question, Jenna smiled back just as placidly and said, "I thought you and Andy were going to stay at the farm."

Grady quirked his sable brow. "Following you seemed more interesting."

"I'll bet."

Grady smiled at her. "Aren't you going to introduce us to the rest of the family?"

"How did you know who we were?" Kip asked with a frown.

"The pictures in Lamar's study," Grady explained.

"You must be very observant," Leslie said nervously.

"He's a detective with the Philadelphia police force," Jenna said, and Leslie paled even more. "So the only surprise would be if Grady wasn't observant."

"I trust you'll remember that in the future?" Grady said.

Jenna smiled tightly. "Don't count on it," she said tartly. Giving him no chance to retort, she went ahead with the formal introductions. "Kip, Grady Noland. Grady, my brother Kip and his lovely wife Leslie."

Grady nodded at Leslie and shook Kip's hand. "So you're the father," Kip said.

Grady gave Kip a man-to-man glance. "For the record, I would have been here a lot sooner had I just known about the situation."

As Jenna had feared, Kip warmed to Grady's innate sense of responsibility immediately. "Leslie and I tried to get Jenna to tell you," he confided.

"How long have you known?" Grady asked with a frown. Spying Jenna, Andy gurgled and strained toward her.

"Since New Year's Day," Kip admitted. "Leslie and I paid a surprise visit to the farm. We tried to get Jenna to tell Dad, but she refused."

Jenna took Andy into her arms. "Having two people in the family who were hysterical about my being a single mother was more than enough, thank you very much."

Grady raised a brow.

"What she means is we tried to talk some sense into her," Kip corrected. "She knows we've always wanted to adopt."

"Andy is my child, Kip," Jenna said softly, feeling proprietorial again.

"And mine," Grady said.

Jenna's eyes widened. Without proof, Grady was acting as if his paternity was a fact. Could it be that he was listening to his heart, just as she had always wanted him to? Hope swelled in Jenna's heart as Kip looked at them both.

"Then the two of you are going to work things out?" Kip ascertained hopefully.

Grady glanced at Jenna, his expression wary but determined. Jenna had the uneasy feeling that whatever happened, Grady was not going to be very open to compromise. "We'll try," Grady said. To Jenna's disappointment, he promised nothing more.

"YOUR'RE STILL ANGRY with me, aren't you?" Grady said as he fell into step beside her.

Jenna cuddled Andy a little closer. The pink in her cheeks grew even deeper. "You didn't have to follow me all the way to Albany."

Grady steered Jenna past the crowds gathering near the baggage claim and out the front doors of the airport toward the parking lot. The winter air was brisk, and instinctively he drew her and Andy close to his side. "How else was I going to know what you were up to?" Grady asked. That morning, before the furniture arrived, he'd been coming downstairs to tell her that the doctors at Pinehaven had substantiated every single word Jenna said. Not content to leave it there, Grady had then called the hospital accreditation board. A person there had confirmed that Pinehaven was a highly respected, if very private and very expensive, medical facility. Grady was almost ready to take Jenna's story as gospel truth—until she had lied to him about going in to Albany to mail a couple of Federal

Express packages. Then his doubts had surfaced all over again. Clearly, she was the wiliest, most determined woman he had ever been around, and that included Clarissa.

Jenna struggled to turn the collar up on her long, jade green reefer with her free hand. "What makes you think I'm up to anything?"

Grady reached over and gave Jenna a hand with the part of the collar she couldn't reach. As he tugged it up, the back of his hand inadvertently brushed the softness of her cheek. Grady dropped his hand quickly. He didn't want to get distracted here. "The guilty look on your face when you saw I had followed you, for one thing," he said. She'd been panicked to see him there, and he'd known she felt she had something to hide.

Jenna's pretty lips set as she marched across the parking lot to her red Volvo station wagon. "I have nothing to feel guilty about, Grady."

Grady figured he would worry about getting his car later. Right now, he wasn't letting her out of his sight. He climbed in the passenger side while Jenna settled Andy in his baby seat. "*Au contraire,* babe. You've got plenty to feel guilty about, but we won't go into that now."

Jenna finished buckling Andy in. She smiled at him and closed the door. "And I suppose you think your conscience is completely free," she retorted as she settled behind the wheel.

"Freer than yours," Grady agreed. While Jenna started the car and adjusted the heater, he moved his seat back to the farthest position. His knees were still touching the dashboard in front of him. Stretching an arm out along the seat, he swiveled to face her, "Anything else you want to do while we're here in Albany?"

Jenna gave her total attention to her driving as she backed out of the space. "I need to stop by the store and pick up a few groceries. So I'll drop you at your car, wherever you parked it, and—"

"No need for that," Grady said cheerfully. "I'll just ride along with you and Andy."

"Look, you can't just leave it here."

"Sure I can," he said easily.

Jenna paused at the end of the row of cars, her foot on the brake. She looked at him in growing frustration. "I have a lot of errands to do here, Grady. I need to go to the dry cleaner and the office supply store, too."

"Then you'll need me along, won't you, in case Andy gets fussy?"

Jenna sighed, but was unable to dispute that.

"Don't worry. We can stop by to pick up my car before we head back to Hudson Falls. But then we'll need to be getting back to the farm."

It was Jenna's turn to narrow her eyes at him suspiciously. "Why?"

Grady didn't know how she could have forgotten—he sure hadn't. "The results of the blood tests are supposed to come in today," he reminded her softly. "Phil General said they'd call us there when they did."

"LISTEN, MR. TITLEMAN—" Grady said.

"Fikleman, Martin Fikleman," the lab technician corrected.

"Are you absolutely sure about what you just told me?" Grady asked. He felt numb with disbelief.

"Positive, Mr. Noland. The results came in today."

"Is it possible," Grady said slowly, "that there could have been some mistake? Some mislabeling or—"

"I handled the lab specimens myself," Martin Fikleman replied. "Everything was done very carefully."

"Then perhaps there was a mistake in the way the DNA test was conducted," Grady said, beginning to feel a little desperate. There had to be. Andy was his child. His and Jenna's. Not his and Clarissa's.

"There was no mistake," Martin Fikleman replied steadfastly. "DNA tests are very accurate at establishing paternity."

"Have you called my ex-wife?" Grady asked. God, this was a nightmare.

"I'm about to."

"What about Ms. Sullivan? Have you told her yet?"

"No, sir. If there's nothing else . . ."

"Actually, there is," Grady was quick to add. "You can fax me those results." Quickly, he read Martin the number of Jenna's fax machine. "I want to see them with my own eyes."

"Yes, sir," Martin said. "Right away."

Grady hung up the phone. He felt like he wanted to punch something. Why? Because he'd done the unthinkable and let his emotions get in the way of his investigation into Andy's paternity. He'd paid little attention to Clarissa's claims and given literally all his attention to Jenna's. Not because one woman's claims were more meritous, but because of what he wanted, deep down. And what he wanted was for Andy to be Jenna's child. Jenna's and his.

And after talking to the officials at Pinehaven, meeting Kip and Leslie and hearing how they'd seen Jenna's baby on New Year's Day, he had come to believe that Andy probably was his child. He had believed it so much that he had expected the DNA results to verify it.

"Grady? Is everything okay?" Jenna asked anxiously from the doorway to her office.

"Why wouldn't it be?" Grady sat back uneasily and folded his arms in front of him.

Without warning, Jenna turned white as a ghost. "I don't know." She wet her lips nervously. "You just don't look very happy."

"That's because I'm not," Grady muttered, his anger, his sense of betrayal building to typhoon force. Right now, he wasn't sure of anyone or anything. Both women had birth certificates for Andy, but Jenna's were in a false name, and Clarissa's were in her real name. Clarissa had gained ten pounds, whereas Jenna was just as willowy as always. Clarissa seemed exactly the type to desert a baby on a doorstep. Jenna seemed the antithesis. And yet Jenna had been the first to demand a blood test.

If the lab results were flawed, and Andy really was his and Jenna's child, as Jenna kept insisting, then Jenna was not only perfectly sane, she was acting just as fiercely protective as any mother would act in a similarly crazy situation. And Grady loved and admired Jenna for that.

If, however, the lab results were true... then Andy was not her child, but his child and Clarissa's. And if that was the case, then whose baby had Jenna been pregnant with last fall? And where was that baby now? Was it possible Jenna had lost her baby during a home birth, then gone into some sort of mental breakdown and kidnapped Clarissa's child? He'd seen cases like that before, where women grieving for a lost child stole into hospital nurseries and took a baby to replace the one they'd lost, not realizing what they were doing.

Was that what had happened to Jenna? And if it turned out it had, how would he cope with that?

"What's coming through on the fax?" Jenna asked as her machine began spitting out paper.

"Phil General is faxing us the results of the blood tests."

Jenna looked perplexed. "Why didn't they just tell you over the phone?" she asked.

"They did, but I want the results in writing and I want them in writing now," Grady said.

Jenna narrowed her eyes at him, swiftly came to her own heart-rending conclusions and beat Grady to the fax. Together, each holding one side of the fax paper, they stared down at the results. Jenna blinked. And blinked again. "It can't be," she breathed incredulously, looking as if she might faint at any second. "It just can't be."

Grady stared at her fiercely. She seemed genuinely stunned.

Almost immediately, Jenna's phone began to ring. His eyes still on her face, Grady beat her to the desk and snatched the receiver from its cradle. His frown deepened as soon as he heard who was at the other end of the line. "Yes, we got 'em. No. *Don't come out here, Clarissa.* I know. Clarissa, listen to me. I'll take care of everything here. You just sit tight. Yes. First thing tomorrow." He hung up the phone and was caught off guard when Jenna flew at him and pounded on his chest.

"You bastard! You set me up!"

He grabbed her fists and held them tightly in front of him. "If anyone was set up, it was me," he said angrily. Furthermore, he'd had about all the manipulating he could take, from both women.

"Like hell!" Jenna struggled against his grip and swore hotly, "I never conspired to take your child away from you."

"Oh, didn't you?" he shot back in a silky voice. "Then what do you call never telling me you were pregnant?" If, indeed, Jenna had been pregnant with his child.

Her soft body trembled against the length of his. Her dark green eyes widened as Grady backed toward the desk and sat down on the edge of it.

"So this is what—payback?" She stepped between his spread knees. Her eyes glimmered with unshed tears that under any other circumstances would have broken his heart. "You want me to know how it feels to have my child stolen from me, not once, but twice?" She slammed her palms against his chest, then spun away from him.

She got as far as the outside of his knees when he grabbed her shirt and pulled her back to him.

"Wait a minute, Jenna." She lost her balance, and her gently rounded bottom made contact with the hardness of his thigh. "I had nothing to do with the kidnapping," he said.

Her attention caught, Jenna folded her arms in front of her, and for a moment she stayed where she was. Her chin took on a stubborn tilt. "How do I know that?"

It irritated Grady to have his integrity questioned. "Because I said so."

"It seems to me I said this was my baby and you didn't believe me."

Grady decided it was altogether too cozy, having her sit on even half his lap. He lifted her away from him, stood and circled the desk. He offered her his back as he poured himself a swallow of brandy. "That was different."

"How?"

Grady lifted the glass to his lips and took a slow sip. His eyes on hers, he said bluntly, "There was factual evidence to the contrary."

Jenna regarded him cantankerously, refusing to back down. "Well, those blood tests you fixed are factual evidence, too." Her green eyes focused on his with absolute purpose. "I want them done again, Grady."

Grady was getting very tired of playing games. He was also very tired of hotly desiring a woman he had no business wanting. "For what purpose?" he asked wearily.

"For the purpose of ascertaining the truth!" Jenna said.

Grady tore his eyes from the flushed contours of her face and finished the brandy in his glass. "All right, we'll redo the lab tests," he relented, hoping, like Jenna, that they'd show a different result. Grady sighed and rubbed the back of his neck. "But if the second set of tests turns out the way the first set did, then I want something from you, too," he finished reluctantly.

"What?" Jenna's voice was soft again, and very wary.

Grady put his glass down and turned to look at her. Damn, but she was beautiful in the soft glow of the fading daylight with her hair all mussed, her eyes bright and sparkling. He didn't want to say it, but he knew for their own peace of mind they had to be sure. "Then I want you to agree to be evaluated by a psychologist friend of mine, Jenna. And don't look at me that way. I'm not doing this to punish you."

Jenna blinked and looked like she was going to cry again. "Then why?"

Grady drew a deep breath. "Because I care about you, Jenna," he said softly, meaning it.

Jenna was silent a long, depressed minute. Grady kept quiet, too. He wished the lab tests had turned out differently. But they hadn't. And it was time he stopped being ruled by his emotions and let himself be guided by the facts. Finally, she swept a hand through her hair, tousling the already mussed strawberry blond waves. "Listen, Grady, if the results come out the same way—and there's no way that will happen if they're done correctly this time—then I'll do what you ask and get evaluated."

Grady breathed a sigh of relief. He had half expected Jenna to fight him on this. It surprised him she hadn't.

"FORGET IT, GRADY, I'm not going to agree to another blood test!" Clarissa shouted into the phone. "I agreed to the first one. I proved what I had to prove. Now I want you and the baby back!"

The baby, Grady thought, latching onto his difficult ex-wife's every word. Not *my* baby, but *the* baby. Warning bells went off in his head. Maybe Jenna was right to want another test. *Maybe there had been a mistake.*

"Look, I just want to be sure," Grady soothed.

"Why can't you be sure now?" Clarissa asked.

Because I want Andy to be Jenna's child, Grady thought. Because Jenna acted more like a mother than Clarissa ever would. And that, in turn, made him hope—against the current physical evidence to the contrary—that there had been a mistake in the DNA tests and that Andy might really be his child and Jenna's. "Are you going to cooperate or not?"

"No way," Clarissa said.

"Fine," Grady said. "Only Jenna and I will need to retest anyway, to insure her peace of mind."

Clarissa sighed. "You're really going through with a second DNA test?"

"Just to be sure, yes," Grady said.

"Then I'll be there, too," Clarissa promised reluctantly.

Grady hung up the phone to find Jenna watching him. "It's all arranged," he said. "Clarissa will meet us in Albany tomorrow. We'll have the blood tests redone first thing tomorrow morning, and shipped out from there to a university hospital in New York City that does DNA testing."

Jenna nodded her understanding. Her relief was palpable. Grady, too, began to relax. Dinner was surprisingly pleasant under the circumstances, and they shared the clean-up efforts. When Andy woke, needing to be changed and fed, Grady helped out with that, too. For once, Jenna seemed content to let Grady handle the bulk of the baby's care.

"Look, if you'll excuse me, I'm going to turn in for the night," she said with a polite smile. "Tomorrow's already shaping up to be a full day, and I'm really beat."

Grady was reluctant to see her go, but he understood. It had been a grueling day. And because Jenna had been up much of the previous night working, she hadn't had a lot of sleep. "I'll play with Andy until he's sleepy again, and then put him down for the night."

"Thanks." Jenny gave Grady a distracted smile, then turned and went up the stairs.

Grady had fun with Andy, but by nine Andy was fast asleep. Grady put him down for the night. Jenna's bedroom door was closed. He could hear her shower running in the bathroom beyond. He went downstairs. It was only nine o'clock. The night stretched out ahead of him endlessly.

Restless, he got up and went into the kitchen. For lack of anything else to do, he brewed a fresh pot of coffee and unloaded the clean dishes from the dishwasher. By the time he'd finished, he could hear Jenna moving around quietly on the second floor, and knew she was out of the shower and wasn't any sleepier than he was.

She just hadn't wanted to spend any more time with him. He could understand that. He had upset her life terribly, just as she had upset his. Last week his life had seemed problem-free. This week it seemed like one big problem. But soon they would have all the answers. Grady would deal with the facts, make his decisions based on those facts, and go from there.

Chapter Ten

Jenna tiptoed down the back stairs, being careful to move soundlessly in the darkness. The blue numbers on the microwave clock flashed 1:37. She only had two more loads to go, and then she'd get the baby.

She didn't want to run away, but when she had learned of the results of the first DNA tests she had swiftly realized she had no choice. It didn't really matter anymore who was conspiring to take her child from her. She only knew someone was. And if she didn't get away from here—now—she would lose her baby again.

She set her suitcases down and opened the back door. Carefully, she moved her belongings across the threshold, then shut the door behind her. Tiptoeing out to the car, she set the two suitcases next to the crib, blankets, diapers and toys. Now all she had to do was get enough food from the kitchen to last for a few days, go in and get Andy, stop by the cash machine in Albany, and she'd be all set.

Jenna shut the trunk, then moved soundlessly across the drive, up the steps and into the kitchen. She was just reaching for the refrigerator door handle when the light flicked on. "Going somewhere?" Grady asked in a cool, deliberate tone.

Jenna sucked in a breath. She turned to face him, making her expression as normal as she could make it, considering that he was glowering at her in a completely uncivilized manner. "Grady. What are you doing up?" Jenna asked cheerfully.

Like Jenna, he was completely dressed in jeans, shirt and blazer, socks and shoes. Unlike Jenna, he did not have on a winter coat. *He* wasn't planning on going anywhere.

He reached behind her and helped her off with her coat. "I thought I might ask you the same thing," he drawled mildly. His sweeping glance covered her from head to foot. "What are you doing up at this hour?"

Jenna swallowed hard. Experience had taught her that emotional arguments with Grady usually ended in a few hot kisses, or at least a sexy clinch. She could not afford to indulge in a few hot kisses. She dropped her gloves and her car keys on the countertop beside her as if she hadn't a care in the world. "Well, actually it's a really funny story," she fibbed.

Grady folded his arms, the action serving only to more distinctly outline the hard, masculine contours of his shoulders and chest beneath his powder blue oxford cloth shirt. His gaze narrowed as Jenna stalked to the cupboard in an effort to buy herself time to come up with said story. Aware of his eyes sliding impatiently over her, she took out a glass, filled it with water from the tap and drank deeply.

"So go ahead," he prodded mercilessly. "I'd like to hear it."

Jenna blew out an uneasy breath and took another drink. "I had a dream." She paused and wet her lips. Pushing her hair away from her face with a careless sweep of her hand, she continued easily, "I guess I must've been sleepwalking—"

"You always sleepwalk fully dressed with a coat on and a suitcase in each hand?" Grady walked forward until he was standing right next to her. He extended one hand, palm flat, to the cabinet beside her as he waited for her answer.

Hellfire and damnation. Now what was she going to do? She had half the baby stuff loaded in the car. Andy was still upstairs. There was no way she could still run away, and no way she could pretend she hadn't been trying to run away...

Jenna wet her lips and tried to look suitably subdued. Telling herself it was imperative she keep a grip on herself, she forced herself to return Grady's level gaze with a flippant one of her own. "I'm a very efficient sleepwalker," she said.

Grady lifted his hand from the cabinet. "And you keep forgetting I'm a cop," he growled, as he stepped back slightly. "I can tell when people are lying to me. Admit it, Jenna." He gave her a once-over that was anything but comforting. "You were trying to run away just now. And you were planning to take Andy with you!"

Jenna ignored the way his dark, dangerous, oh-so-male presence was suddenly looming over her. "All right. I admit it." Jenna set her glass on the counter with a thud. "I was running away, but only because you left me no choice!"

"Really." His eyes steady, Grady sauntered closer and picked up the glass she had set down. He took a long, thirsty drink, draining it, and then fixed her with a laser-sharp gaze that let her know she was in trouble. "And how," he said politely, "do you figure that?"

Jenna refilled the glass, then took another gulp to calm her nerves. She forced herself to meet his eyes. "Someone screwed up those blood tests, Grady. The more I think about it, the more I'm convinced it wasn't an accident."

Suddenly, the troubled light was back in his eyes. Grady released an aggravated breath and shoved a hand through his tousled, sable brown hair. "Well, we'll know shortly, won't we?"

Jenna shrugged, wishing she had Grady's faith in the system. But in the last two plus weeks, the system had done nothing but betray her. "Maybe we will and maybe we won't." She blew out a weary breath. "If the DNA results were screwed up once, they could be screwed up again." The question was, Jenna thought, by whom?

He studied her with resigned disapproval, guessing accurately where this conversation was leading. He braced a hand on either side of her. "Jenna, if I wanted to take the baby from you, I have all the evidence I need right now to do just that."

"Then why don't you?" she demanded emotionally.

Grady leaned closer in a drift of brisk, masculine cologne. The shadow of his evening beard clung to his face, giving him an even more rugged look than usual. "Because I want to be sure I'm doing the right thing if and when it comes to that, and right now I'm not sure of anything," Grady said softly. "Except that you need me and will continue to need me until this whole mess is resolved."

Tears of gratitude and frustration pooled in her eyes. She willed them not to fall, but they fell anyway. Jenna turned her back to him and felt her shoulders graze the hardness of his chest. "I see."

He put his hands on her shoulders and wordlessly turned her gently around to face him. His eyes softened as they searched her upturned face. "Do you?" he asked quietly, abruptly looking and acting as vulnerable to the fates that were conspiring against them as she felt. "I want to help you, Jenna. I want to be here for you—if you'll let me."

When he looked at her like that, when he touched her so tenderly, it was all she could do not to fall in love with him. Hanging on to her self-preservation by a thread, she shrugged free of his light, detaining grip. "I'm tired of talking about this, Grady. I'm going to bed."

He stepped in front of her, barring her way to the stairs. The implacable look was back on his face. "Not alone, you're not."

Jenna's heart skipped several beats. She swallowed around the sudden dryness in her throat. This was the dangerous side of Grady, and the one she found most appealing. "Come on, Grady," she forced herself to say wryly. "Give me a break. I'm not going to try to run away again."

"I know you're not, because this time I'm not letting you out of my sight," he countered with a knowing smile. Hand beneath her elbow, he guided her toward the stairs.

Jenna dug in her heels and grabbed the banister. She refused to go up even one step. "This is ridiculous."

"I agree," he said mildly, extricating her hand from the banister, "but I didn't start it with my sleepwalking routine."

She studied him in exasperation. He was so sure he was doing the right thing! Her chest and throat so congested with emotion that she could barely breathe, Jenna backed up until she felt her spine graze the wall. She forced herself to cross her arms and lean against the wall insouciantly. Aware he, too, was plotting his next move, she angled her chin up another notch. "Well, if you trust me so little, I want to know why you don't just take the baby everyone already agrees is yours and leave." They both knew he would have no trouble overpowering her physically, and with the evidence they had gathered so far, he could probably get the law on his side, too.

Grady propped his hands on his hips and glared at her in aggravation. "Several reasons. One, you seem to need to be near Andy for your own peace of mind."

That was certainly true, Jenna thought.

"Two—" he patiently closed the distance between them "—I don't think it'd be a good idea for you to be alone out here."

Jenna didn't want Grady's protection. She wanted his unerring trust. She glowered at him stubbornly and wished he hadn't chosen to stand so close to her. "Why not?"

"Because you're going through a difficult time, that's why not," Grady explained.

"So why not foist me off on family and friends and take off?" Jenna continued, forcing herself to be logical and cool, despite the fact she could feel the warmth emanating from his tall, muscled body beckoning to her like a soft, cozy feather bed.

"Because I care about what happens to you," Grady said gruffly. "And my gut instinct tells me that you've got feelings for me, too."

His gut instinct was right. And that frightened her more than the botched-up DNA tests. "I told you I wasn't looking for a relationship!" Jenna stormed. And particularly not with a man who was so much like her overly suspicious ex-husband. She couldn't go through life having to prove herself and her intentions at every turn.

"Well, that's too bad because, like it or not, I'm here. And I do care about you. As a friend. And maybe—" his voice lowered another notch as he planted a hand on either side of her "—more than that."

She saw the change in his eyes and drew back, shaken and confused. "How do you expect me to trust that?" His caring what happened to her, or the baby, hadn't helped her so far!

Grady gathered her into his arms and brought her against him. "Because it's real," he said softly, the passion in his low voice fueling her own. "Just like what we feel every time we look at each other is real, too. You can call it whatever you want, Jenna." He lifted a hand to her hair and sifted through the silky strands. "You can label it or not. But it's there."

"That's not the way it is at all!"

"Tell me that after I've kissed you, and I'll believe you." Engulfing her with the heat and strength of his body from head to toe, he lowered his head and delivered a breath-stealing kiss.

Jenna meant to fight him, she swore she would, but at the first touch of his mouth to hers, she trembled, and a low moan issued from her throat. She tingled everywhere they touched and everywhere they didn't. A melting weakness shifted through her, further weakening her resolve. He felt so good against her, so warm and strong and solid. So male. And it had been such a long time since he had made love to her, she thought wistfully. Such a long, long time since she'd felt beautiful and wanted, soft and feminine.

Grady unbuttoned as he kissed. His mouth still moving ardently over hers, he divested her of her blazer and blouse, and then her bra. Jenna offered no assistance or resistance as his hands cupped her breasts. It was everything she could do to try to hold herself and her soaring feelings in check. But when he uttered a soft, male groan of contentment as he brushed her hardening nipples with his fingertips, then bent to kiss the taut, aching crowns, desire swept through her in powerful waves. "Oh, God, Grady," she whispered.

"I know," he said, taking her breasts greedily into his hands and backing her up against the wall again.

He was hard as a rock against her. Demanding. Coaxing response after response from her with his deep, drugging kisses. Dizzy, overcome with need and yearning, she tugged the shirt from the waistband of his pants and slid her hands up the solid warmth of his back. The world had narrowed to just the two of them. All she knew, all she wanted to know at that moment, was that his skin was smooth and hot to the touch, corded with muscle. And she wanted more, so much more than a few kisses and the feel of his hands on her breasts. She wanted to know all of him, just as she wanted him to know all of her. She wanted to feel connected to him again, not just physically, but heart and soul.

Without breaking the kiss, he found the front zipper of her jeans and pushed them down over her hips to her knees. Impatient to be free of them, to tear down the emotional and physical boundaries she had imposed around herself, Jenna kicked them the rest of the way off. For the second time in her life, she was going to enjoy without worrying about the consequences. Clad only in panties, her heart pounding, she divested him of his jeans. And his Jockey shorts.

He stroked her softly through the cloth, swiftly raising her desire to a fever pitch. She moaned her frustration, and then her panties were off, too. He was straining against her, moving inside her, letting her know he wanted her as wildly as she wanted him. Pushing herself up a little higher, she arched her back and pulled him deeper still. That quickly, they catapulted over the edge. Shuddering, their breathing rough and noisy, they clung together.

"Jenna." His voice was rough against her ear, filled not with regret, as she had feared, but longing for more.

She swallowed hard as yet another thrill swept through her, tightening her breasts, weakening her knees. Her mouth was swollen from his. She could feel it, even as she longed for his kiss again. She wanted him that way, all fire and passion, no holds barred, nothing standing between them. Not the baby, not his work, not his crazy notions about cops being unmarriageable.

Maybe she had been wrong, she thought. Maybe she should have told him about the pregnancy, given him the chance to be a proper father to Andy from the very first. But it was too late now... wasn't it? Or was it?

He threaded his hands through her hair, pushing it away from her ear. "I want you upstairs," he said softly, "in my bed." And what Grady wanted, it seemed, he got. The next thing Jenna knew, she was being swept up into his arms and carried up the back stairs. Dropping her into the rumpled covers of his bed, he joined her swiftly. They kissed hotly, possessively, the passion so strong and so right and so total, it didn't feel quite real. But it was, Jenna thought, as Grady's hands swept down her body once again. It was.

AFTERWARD, they lay tangled together, their intertwined bodies exhausted, trembling, and yet still eager for more.

"I thought I had imagined how good it was," Grady said, pressing a kiss against her bare shoulder. "I didn't." He sighed his contentment and held her closer yet.

Spent, Jenna lay in Grady's arms. Now that the passion had faded, reality was beginning to return. She didn't want to lose her baby. She knew Grady would only believe her if the second DNA tests supported instead of disputed her claims. So why was she still here with him? Why had she allowed herself to make love with him that way? She had so much more common sense than that... except that Grady had gotten to a place deep inside her heart that no one had ever even come close to before. He'd made her want to lose herself completely in him, and in their lovemaking, and that frightened her. It frightened her a lot.

"I wonder what you're thinking," Grady drawled.

"I'm wondering how it is that we keep finding ourselves in these messes," she lamented wryly. Because it wasn't like her, it wasn't like her at all!

Grady groaned with comic effect, as if he understood perfectly and wondered the same. He rubbed his hand up and down her arm, from shoulder to wrist, creating frissons of warmth everywhere he touched. "Ever hear the word irresistible?" he teased, rolling so that she was beneath him once again.

The solid feel of him sent another thrill of excitement rushing up her spine. "Yes."

He framed her face with his hands and gazed lovingly down into her face. "Well, that's what you are to me," he whispered softly, looking as completely and utterly besotted as she felt whenever he touched her. "Completely irresistible."

Jenna released a wavering sigh. "To me, too," she said finally, then bit her lip. "Not that I think that is good," she amended cautiously, beginning to feel more like her normal self now that his kisses had stopped. "It's not."

Grady acknowledged her continuing reservations with a lift of his brow. "Yeah, but it felt good at the time." Grady rolled so that she was on top of him. "And I'm willing to bet it could feel good again," he said softly, as he began to make love to her once more.

An hour later, Jenna finally slept, her soft, warm body curled against Grady's side. Grady lay on his back, staring at the ceiling. Jenna had been right. They shouldn't have made love. Not now. Not until everything was settled, and maybe not even then.

He couldn't make too much of Clarissa's reluctance to take a second blood test. And the way Clarissa kept referring to Andy as "the baby" and not "my baby" meant nothing except Clarissa was not going to be much of a parent. But baby or no, Grady knew he was not going back to Clarissa. Their marriage was over. He was not going to resurrect it.

As for Jenna...

She was a loving and attentive mother. Andy clearly adored her. Grady could see the two of them parenting Andy together. Was that, plus his desire for Jenna, clouding his perspective? he wondered uncomfortably. Making him miss clues he should have seen?

What if they retook the blood tests and the DNA results were the same? he wondered uneasily. What if it was necessary for Grady to take Jenna to see his psychologist friend at the department, and she pronounced Jenna completely loony? Could the unthinkable be true? Was he falling head over heels in love with a crazy person?

And what would he do if he was? He knew the answer to that. If that was the case, if Jenna needed help, then he'd stay with her and see that she got it.

But he didn't think that was the case. The fact of the matter was Jenna was too lucid, too loving, too determined and forthright, to be delusional. The truth was as she'd said. Andy was Jenna's child, and he'd been taken from her. It was up to Grady to prove an abduction had occurred, he thought, and then see that it didn't happen again, that both Andy and Jenna remained safe.

After that... Grady sighed. As far as he and Jenna went, they would just have to see what was possible. She kept insisting that she wasn't looking for either a relationship or marriage, and if he was completely honest, neither was he. Because frankly, he wasn't sure it was possible to be a good cop and be married.

Grady frowned. He didn't want to be without Jenna, either. Didn't want to live in two different states while they split the care of an infant son. Nor was he willing to give up his job with the Philadelphia police force. And he doubted Jenna would leave her home in New York and relocate for his convenience. So where did that leave them? he wondered. Just what kind of resolution was going to be possible here?

Chapter Eleven

"The baby's awake," Grady said softly, several hours later.

"I know," Jenna said. She could hear Andy in his crib. He was gurgling happily, probably either to the mobile that hung overhead or to one of the dolls he had brought back with him from his stay at Alec's and Jack's.

"He's going to need a bottle, isn't he?"

Jenna nodded.

"I'll go down and warm one, then," Grady said. He flung back the sheets and headed for the stairs.

Jenna shrugged on her robe. She went in to Andy, knowing he'd be wet. By the time she had changed him and put on a fresh sleeper, Grady was upstairs with the formula. "Bring Andy in here with us," Grady said. Bottle in hand, he beckoned toward the rumpled covers on Jenna's bed.

Jenna settled against the pillows Grady had propped against the headboard. Andy cradled in her arms, she proceeded to feed him his bottle as Grady watched.

Grady smiled and tickled Andy beneath the chin. Andy stopped nursing and gurgled wildly, looking thoroughly amused and thoroughly content. Jenna felt pangs of regret and longing simultaneously. It would be so nice to have more times like this. Lazy mornings, with Grady and their baby. She wanted the sense of connectedness and affection and solidarity that only family could provide. Jenna looked at Andy's wide blue eyes, so much like his father's, and wondered in frustration why Grady couldn't just see that Andy was their son, and no one else's.

Grady paused and reached out to touch a lock of her tousled strawberry blond hair. "Last night was great, Jenna." He probed her eyes. "The question is, where do we go from here?"

I wish I knew, Jenna thought. "Isn't this conversation a little premature?" she asked lightly.

Grady regarded his son fondly. He let Andy wrap his tiny fist around one of his fingers, then turned to Jenna and saw the indecision in her eyes. "I'm not giving the baby up, Jenna," Grady warned quietly.

Jenna sat Andy up and patted him on the back. "I thought you said cops made lousy husbands and lousy fathers."

"Maybe I could be the exception to the rule this time. I'm willing to try," Grady said softly, holding her gaze. "Mind if I feed him the second half of his bottle?"

"Not at all," Jenna said. This was the way it should be—two parents, equally shared responsibilities. A sense of family and love...

Jenna watched as Grady settled Andy on his lap. Andy tapped his fingers on the bottle as he sucked down his breakfast. "Supposing we get everything worked out," Grady continued casually. "Would you marry me?"

Jenna had longed to hear those words from him for months now. Ever since she had found out they were going to have a child together, she had dreamed about those words, yearned for them, wished for them. But the reality fell short of her imaginings, maybe because she knew Grady would never be proposing if she hadn't had his child.

Jenna's shoulders tensed. Her heart reverberated with hurt. With effort, she blinked back the hot, bitter tears gathering behind her eyes and kept her voice coolly matter-of-fact as she replied, "I don't want your charity, Grady."

"Then think of our baby, Jenna." Grady linked his fingers with hers. "Andy needs two parents."

Jenna withdrew her hand from his. "I married for the wrong reason once, Grady," she reminded him stiffly. "I'm not doing it again."

They were silent for a minute. Jenna swallowed hard around the fear gathering deep inside her. "Grady, what happens if the test comes out wrong again?"

The planes of his face seemed to sharpen. His slate-blue eyes grew more alert. "What makes you think it will?"

Jenna paused, feeling treacherously near tears again. "The fact it was already messed with or switched once." Grady made no comment about her assumption. But something in him seemed to harden. Suddenly, he looked more suspicious Philly cop than contented lover.

"There's still Nanny Beth's testimony," he said. "The guys in the department are getting close to finding her."

"When do you think we'll be able to talk to her?" Jenna asked.

"I hope before the day is done," Grady said.

"THANK GOODNESS that's over," Clarissa exclaimed at Albany Memorial Hospital. "Again."

Grady sent Clarissa a censuring look. "I'll bring the car around," he told Jenna.

Jenna nodded. "I'll be out as soon as I change Andy's diaper," she promised, then disappeared into the powder room. When she emerged minutes later, she saw Clarissa chatting with Baxter. It was no surprise they'd run into her ex-husband. Jenna knew he was on staff and had patients at all the area hospitals. But it was a shock to see him looking so chummy with Clarissa.

She waited around until the conversation had apparently run its course, then caught up with Baxter.

"What was all that about?" Jenna asked as she fell into step beside Baxter, Andy cradled in her arms.

"In a nutshell, she wants me to work on you so she'll have a clear path to Grady herself," Baxter said. He gave Jenna a hard look. "I'd do it, too, if I thought I had half a chance."

Jenna felt a tinge of regret. Despite everything that had passed between them, she had never wanted to hurt Baxter. "We never should've married, Baxter," she said gently. "You know that."

"I know you think so," Baxter said stiffly.

"I don't love you."

Baxter shoved his hands in the pockets of his starched white lab coat. "Do you love Detective Noland?"

The fifty-million-dollar question. "I don't know," Jenna said evasively. Though inwardly she thought maybe she did, she just didn't want to admit it to herself.

"Yeah, right," Baxter said skeptically.

Jenna caught sight of Grady's car waiting in front of the hospital. "I've got to go." She put Andy's knit cap on his head and headed out the door.

"What took so long?" Grady asked as Jenna settled Andy in his car seat, strapped him in and then got in the car herself.

Jenna twisted toward Grady as she fastened her shoulder harness. "I saw my ex talking to your ex and I wanted to check it out."

Grady rested one hand on the wheel. He made no effort to put the car in gear, just looked at her closely. "You think they're up to something?"

Seeing Clarissa and Baxter together had struck a chord in Jenna. "Has it occurred to you that the two of them might have gotten together and kidnapped Andy?"

Grady's suspicious look deepened. "In order to keep us apart?"

Jenna shrugged, wishing Grady hadn't shaved quite so closely that morning. "Something like that."

His eyes never leaving hers, Grady thought about it a moment. "Did Baxter know that we were together last spring?"

"Not that I know of, but... He could have had me followed, Grady. Just as your ex could have had us followed, and anyone who had followed us from that party at Alec's that night would have known I spent the night at your place."

Grady frowned, but didn't disagree with her. "While you were having your blood taken, I had a chance to talk to Clarissa out in the hall."

"What did she say?"

"That this second test was just a formality. We'd only end up finding out what we already knew. She wants me to go ahead and marry her again, for the baby's sake."

"And?" Jenna waited for his answer with bated breath.

"I told her it was over between us, no matter who Andy's mother is," he finally said.

"Even if Clarissa was Andy's mother, you wouldn't marry her?" Jenna asked as hope for her future flared inside her. Maybe Grady did care about her, after all!

"Why? We'd only get divorced again, probably even more acrimoniously than the last time. Clarissa and I are not compatible. You and I are, Jenna."

Jenna drew an unsteady breath and ducked her head. He hadn't said he loved her yet. But he was on the right track.

"What about you? I saw you talking to Baxter. Has this business with Andy given you second thoughts about your divorce?" Grady asked.

Jenna shook her head, her opinion on that unchanged. "I told Baxter there was no hope for us getting back together," Jenna admitted.

"And?"

"As with your ex, the news seems to be very slow sinking in," Jenna said.

"ANY MESSAGES?" Grady asked the moment they arrived at her Hudson Falls farmhouse, settled a sleeping Andy in his crib and went to the first floor.

Jenna went into her study and checked her telephone answering machine. "Mostly work messages," she proclaimed after several minutes of listening.

Grady came in carrying a tray of coffee, cups and a plate of shortbread cookies and fresh fruit. He looked disappointed. "Anything else?" He poured Jenna a cup of coffee, stirred in some hazelnut flavored coffee creamer and handed it to her.

"The receptionist at my dentist's office, telling me it's time for my six month check-up."

"I mean important." Grady poured himself a cup of coffee.

"Nope." Jenna settled on the sofa and began going through the mail that had been delivered in her absence. She and Grady had spent so much time together the last few days, it almost seemed like they were married. It wasn't an unpleasant sensation. Rather she cherished the intimacy in even the simple things. She cherished the time spent with him, and though she knew she was wearing her heart on her sleeve, she couldn't help but wish things continued on in exactly this way.

Jenna had just opened a bill when the phone rang. Because he was closer, Grady picked up the phone. "Grady. Yeah, put her through." He covered the receiver and looked at Jenna. "It's Nanny Beth."

Jenna leaped to her feet. At last, something was going her way! "Put Nanny on the speakerphone," she instructed Grady. "I want to hear this, too."

Grady did as she asked. Seconds later, Nanny Beth's high, thin voice warbled over the long-distance lines. "Jenna, sweetheart?"

Jenna smiled. "Hi, Nanny Beth," she said cheerfully, unable to hide the smile in her voice or the happiness in her heart. "Where are you?"

"In Bermuda. The police here tracked me down and said you wanted to talk to me." Nanny Beth paused a disapproving moment. "What's going on there, sweetie?"

"It's a long story, Nanny Beth, but I've got a policeman here with me, a Detective Grady Noland from the Philadelphia police force. He wants you to tell him how and when and where Andy was born."

"No hints," Grady mouthed to Jenna.

Jenna released a slow breath. Suddenly, she was very worried. What if Nanny Beth said the wrong thing, or in some way made Grady think he had been misled?

"You mean you want me to tell him how Laura Johnson stayed with you last fall and had a baby in Hudson Falls at Christmastime?" Nanny Beth asked anxiously. "And how you helped take care of Andy and then fell in love with him and then found out Laura wanted to give Andy up for adoption, because she didn't think she could care for him properly, so you told her you'd care for him, and started making plans to adopt him right away?"

Jenna rolled her eyes. Leave it to Nanny Beth to keep up the ruse past the time when it was necessary. "No, Nanny Beth. I don't want you to tell Grady about the story you and I cooked up to cover my tracks. I want you to tell him the truth, without any more prompting from me."

"All right, dear. Detective Noland, are you there?"

"Right here," Grady affirmed.

"Well, I delivered Jenna's baby. We were supposed to go across the border to Vermont because Jenna wanted to have her baby there. She thought it would be easier to keep the birth private. But her labor came so hard and fast that we didn't even have time to go into Hudson Falls! So I delivered the baby at the farm, and then Dr. Koen came out to make sure Jenna and the baby were all right. He wanted to move them to a hospital, but Jenna didn't want to go, so it ended up being a home birth from start to finish."

Grady breathed a sigh of relief as he realized that Nanny Beth's story matched Jenna's perfectly.

"I understand you finally got everything worked out with your family," Nanny Beth said to Jenna.

"More or less," Jenna said, not about to get into that. "Listen, would you mind cutting your vacation short and coming on home, Nanny Beth? I think I'm going to need you."

"YOU LOOK HAPPY," Jenna told Grady as she hung up the phone. In fact, happy didn't begin to cover it. He looked ecstatic.

"That's because I got my wish," Grady said hoarsely, taking her into the warm circle of his arms. And then his mouth came down on hers.

Jenna's heartbeat pounded like thunder against his as their mouths met with fiery demand. No one had ever wanted her like this, Jenna thought, as his lips caressed hers and his tongue probed languorously deep. She had never wanted like this, never ached so just to be touched, held, loved by a man. But it wasn't just any man she wanted, it was Grady.

He drew away from her. Her breath caught as she gazed into his eyes. As she read his intent, to make love to her here, now, in the study while Andy was still asleep, her heart began a slow, heavy beat. Bending close, he pulled her against his hard length and used his other hand to brush the hair from her nape. His warm breath touched the soft, vulnerable skin of her neck. And then his lips.

Trembling with pent-up desire, Jenna turned her head so their lips met once again. "Oh, Grady," she whispered. *I love you, I love you so much.*

He deepened the kiss and wrapped his arms around her, the pressure of his hands on her hips and back bringing her intimately close. Another torrent of need swept through her, further weakening her knees. Grady backed to the sofa. They went down in a tangle of arms and legs and came together quickly, in an explosion of passion, tenderness and need.

Afterward, replete and drowsy, Jenna melted against Grady in blissful ecstasy. "What are you thinking?" he murmured contentedly, running his fingers through her hair.

Jenna flattened her hands on the muscled warmth of his hair-whorled chest. He was so masculine. So steady, despite all the turmoil of recent days. "I was thinking that I've missed this...missed the closeness—"

"That comes with making love?" Grady asked, caressing her shoulders gently.

"And being with someone so intimately," Jenna admitted as she rested her head against his chest and listened to the steady drumbeat of his heart. She didn't know why she was suddenly being so honest, even if she hadn't exactly come right out and said it was Grady she had missed, not just someone. Anyone. Her emotions were still in turmoil where Grady was concerned. He hadn't said he loved her. Only that he would marry her because of the baby.

"I've missed being with you, too," Grady said. He turned her palm up and pressed a kiss on it.

Jenna snuggled closer. *I need to start appreciating what I have and stop wishing for the impossible,* she thought. "There were so many times I wanted to call you this past year."

Grady's hands swept down her back and tightened on her spine. "Why didn't you?" he said.

Jenna shrugged. *I was afraid it wouldn't work out. I didn't want to be rejected.* Her lips curved wryly. She propped her chin on her fist and looked at Grady honestly. "I didn't want to be told cops and relationships don't mix."

"And now?" Grady asked, tangling his hands in her hair as her lips moved against his throat.

"Now I just want us to forget everything that's happened and start all over again." Jenna kissed his collarbone. "There's only one thing standing in our way," Jenna finished with a sigh. Grady looked at her, and they said in unison, "We've got to find out who kidnapped Andy!"

GALVANIZED INTO ACTION by their mutual concern for their infant son, they dressed quickly. Jenna picked up a blank yellow legal pad and a red felt marking pen from her desk. "Okay. Here are the suspects we've pretty much eliminated so far," she said as she wrote. "My father, my brother Kip and his wife Leslie, and Nanny Beth."

Grady finished buttoning his shirt and began hunting around for his boots. "That leaves Baxter and Clarissa. We disagree about Baxter, but we both agree Clarissa could be capable of just about anything if it enabled her to get what she wanted."

"I seriously doubt Clarissa is going to confess to any wrongdoing, unless we have solid proof against her. How's your partner doing with the phony documents she produced?"

"Still working on tracking down the source."

Jenna frowned. "What do you suggest we do next?"

Grady paced to the carafe of coffee he'd brought in earlier. He was in luck. The coffee was still hot. "I think we should start by putting our emotions aside and running this investigation less like a family drama and more like an official police inquiry." The way he should have run it in the first place, he told himself sternly.

Grady poured himself a cup and promptly downed half of it before continuing, "We've checked for inside clues and found little except that it was an inside job and that no one in the family is confessing to it."

"So now what?" Jenna said, as she helped herself to a cup of coffee.

"Now it's time we checked for outside clues," Grady said.

Chapter Twelve

"Nope, didn't see anything," Jenna's neighbor to the east said.

"Wish I could help you, but I was at my son's elementary school all day helping out with his class's Valentine's Day party," said her neighbor to the north.

"Maybe the third time's the charm," Grady said as he approached.

"Maybe," Jenna said glumly. And maybe they'd never discover anything at all. Maybe the only thing this guest would do was make it look as if she had engineered Andy's abduction from start to finish, just to get Grady's attention and falsely win his sympathy and then his heart. She knew it had occurred to him, just as it occurred to her. She saw it every time she looked into his eyes.

"Now that you mention it, I did notice something," Edward Frick said. A farmer, he was dressed in overalls, a green flannel shirt and work boots. "I drove by about two in the afternoon. I remember, because I was on my way into town to pick up some flowers for my wife, it being Valentine's Day and all, and when I went by your place, Jenna, I saw a man putting a baby in a car seat into the back of a car."

"How could you have seen all that just driving by?" Grady interrupted. "I mean, Jenna's house is pretty far back from the road."

"That's what was so unusual about it," Edward Frick said. "The car wasn't parked next to the house. It was parked at the end of the drive, next to the road, just inside the property line. It just didn't make sense to me to carry the baby and that car seat all the way down the lane on such a cold day, when the driver could easily have pulled the car all the way up to the front porch."

"Unless you were trying not to be heard," Grady muttered.

Jenna looked at Grady. "That explains why I never heard a car. It's nearly half a mile from the end of the drive to the house."

"Did you get a good look at the baby or the person carrying the baby?" Grady asked.

Edward Frick pointed to Andy. "The baby kind of looked like the one you got sleeping in the back of your car right now—leastways, it was about the same size, a real little one. I wasn't close enough to see the baby's face or anything."

No matter, Jenna thought. If there had been a baby outside her farmhouse on Valentine's Day, then it had to be Andy. Now all they had to do was identify the kidnapper. "What kind of car was it?" Jenna asked excitedly. "Do you remember?"

"Sure do, 'cause we don't see many of that kind out here in the country. It was a fancy black Porsche."

His expression all business, Grady pulled a small pad and pen from the inside pocket of his tweed blazer. "Did you get the license plate?" he asked with cool police efficiency.

"No." Edward Frick shook his head in obvious regret. "Sorry."

"Any of the letters on it?" Grady persisted.

"No, not a one, sorry," Edward said.

Despair welled up in Jenna. She pushed it aside determinedly. "Can you give us a description of the man carrying the baby?" she asked.

"Well..." Edward Frick rubbed his bearded jaw. "He was wearing a navy trench coat, the kind that goes over suits."

"What color hair did he have?" Jenna asked.

"Now that I remember. It was dark brown, and he had one of them fancy city-slicker haircuts, the kind that don't seem to move at all in the wind. Oh, and he was clean-shaven, no beard or mustache."

Jenna looked at Grady. There was only one person who wore a navy trench coat and drove a black Porsche who could have had access to the security codes at the Sullivan family farm. Her smile widened. "Bingo," she said.

STEVE JACKSON looked up from the stack of papers on his desk when Grady and Jenna walked in, Andy cradled in Jenna's arms. His smile faded as Grady removed a badge from his pocket and flashed it in Steve's direction. "Mind if we ask you a few questions?" Grady said.

"That depends," Steve said nervously. He looked from Jenna to the baby and at Jenna again. "Jenna?"

"It's okay, Steve," Jenna said gently, sure even if Grady wasn't that no harm had been meant. Steve was too nice a guy to have abducted Andy for malicious or greedy reasons. "We just want to talk," she said.

Steve put down his pen. He studied Jenna's face wordlessly for several seconds, then sighed. "You know, don't you?" he presumed heavily.

Jenna nodded and continued to rub Andy's back. He had just had a bottle and was about to go to sleep again. "We've got an eyewitness who saw you loading Andy into the car midafternoon on Valentine's Day. What I don't understand is why, Steve."

Steve pushed his swivel chair farther from his desk and propped an ankle on the opposite knee. "Isn't it obvious? You and your dad have always been so nice to me. I wanted you to be happy."

"You thought kidnapping her baby would make her happy?" Grady asked gruffly. His expression ominous and unforgiving, he glared at Steve.

"I thought reuniting her and the baby with the baby's father would make her happy," Steve corrected. He got to his feet and shoved his hands in the pockets of his tailored Armani trousers. "And since Jenna was too stubborn to do it on her own..." Steve looked at Grady and frowned. "What I don't get is what *you* have to do with all this," he said.

Grady swore heatedly beneath his breath. "I'm the baby's father," Grady growled.

Steve blanched. "Wait a minute." Steve turned to Jenna. "I thought you were involved with Alec Roman!"

Jenna shook her head. Andy was beginning to feel heavy, so she sat down. This comedy of errors seemed to know no end. "Let's start at the beginning, Steve," she said gently. "How did you know I was pregnant?"

A flush started in Steve's neck and worked its way up to his face. He looked at Jenna. "Remember when I delivered that Christmas gift from your father to the farm on December twentieth and Nanny Beth answered the door?" Jenna nodded. Steve continued, "Well, you were supposed to be in Sweden for the holidays, on business. Only Nanny Beth was supposed to be out at the farm then. But I caught a glimpse of you coming in the back of the house just as I arrived, and I saw how pregnant you were, and... Well, I was worried, so I cornered Nanny Beth and demanded to know what was going on. She told me you were hiding out at the farm, not to recuperate from your divorce from Baxter, as everyone had been purposefully led to believe, but because your baby's father had told you that marriage just wasn't for him. Nanny Beth said she had tried to talk some sense into you, to get you to at least call the baby's father or tell her who it was, but that you stubbornly refused."

"Imagine the trouble you would have saved us all if you'd only listened to Nanny Beth," Grady interjected dryly as he put his pad and pen away.

Jenna shot Grady a silencing look, then turned to Steve. "I still don't get how you figured out it was Alec's baby," she said.

"I didn't. Not right away. I mean, at first I just assumed it had to be Baxter's, because I know you don't play ar—well, never mind."

"We understand she's not promiscuous," Grady said.

Jenna covered Andy's shoulders with a blanket and settled back more comfortably in her chair. "Go on with your story, Steve," she encouraged quietly. "We want to know how and why and when you decided to take the baby to Alec Roman's."

"Well, I kept in touch with Nanny Beth from Christmas on. I called her once a week, usually on some pretense or another, but she knew what I was really worried about was you. And she told me that instead of coming to your senses, as she had hoped you would after Andy's birth, you were being more stubborn than ever. And that you were also pretty depressed about it. She said if she only knew who the father was she'd tell him herself! So, one afternoon at the end of January while you were in Albany on business, I went out to the farm, and she let me go through your office files and calendar. As close as we could figure, you'd been at Alec Roman's party the night Andy was conceived. A glance at your long-distance phone records showed you'd been in constant touch with him by phone ever since. We also knew, from the news reports, what a big playboy he was. So..."

Jenna was so stunned for a moment she couldn't speak. "Are you telling me Nanny Beth was in on the kidnapping?"

"I wanted her to be, but she refused. She said you were going to tell your father February fifteenth, when you went into Albany again on business. I had an idea how Lamar would react to the news, and figured it would be better if you had already reunited with Andy's father before you dropped the news on your dad, so I waited for the first opportunity, and took it."

"How did you know the code to deactivate the alarm?"

"Lamar has it in his office safe, along with a spare key to the front door."

"Oh, Steve." Jenna cuddled the baby sleeping in her arms closer to her chest and shook her head at him in regret.

Steve shot Jenna a penitent look. "I'm *really* sorry, Jenna."

"Why didn't you come forward sooner and tell Jenna what you'd done?" Grady asked. Gliding closer to Andy, he smoothed a palm over Andy's baby-fine hair.

Steve shrugged and looked confused again. "I thought everything had worked out the way it was supposed to. I mean, who'd turn their back on a woman like Jenna if they knew..."

No one, Grady thought. In fact, the more he was with her the more he knew he'd been a fool to ever let her go. Maybe his marriage to Clarissa hadn't worked. It didn't mean his relationship with Jenna wouldn't.

"I'm sorry, Jenna," Steve said contritely. "I was just trying to help. And anyway, I did check with your dad the next day."

Jenna frowned. "What do you mean?"

"I asked Lamar if he had heard from you and he said, and I quote, 'Jenna is fine. She finally came home last night, and as it happens, it wasn't a moment too soon.' I told him I had been worried about you, and he said it was easy to see why. I asked your dad if you had explained everything to him, and he said you had. He also told me not to worry, that he knew I had stumbled on 'quite a bit' when I went out to the farm at Christmas, and again in January, but that he was getting you all the help you needed to see that your situation got squared away once and for all.

"I asked him how long he thought it would take, and he just shrugged and said he hoped everything would be taken care of in a couple of weeks." Steve paused. "I thought everything was fine."

Only it hadn't been, Jenna thought, because Steve had delivered the baby to the wrong man at the wrong address. "I thought Andy had been kidnapped," Jenna said. "I accused my father of doing the kidnapping, and when he denied it, I nearly had a nervous breakdown."

"Oh, God, Jenna, I'm sorry," Steve said, his face ashen.

"I understand you were just trying to help." Jenna sighed. With her free hand, she tucked her hair behind her ear.

"Now I'm confused." Steve paused. "If Alec Roman wasn't Andy's father, why were you in constant touch with him?"

Jenna smiled. "Because last spring Alec agreed to let me use his jet to ferry kids back and forth whenever he wasn't using it."

"Oh." Steve looked more chagrined than ever.

"And at that party I had solicited a rather large donation from him—before I started talking to Grady."

Again, everyone was silent. "Well, at least we have confirmed Andy was kidnapped and no harm was done. Now all we have to do is figure out what happened to the DNA tests," Jenna said.

"I have a feeling I already know the answer to that," Grady said grimly.

"YOU KNOW what you did constitutes fraud," Grady said to Martin Fikleman, the lab tech at Philadelphia General, several hours later, after Martin had admitted switching the results.

"I know. I'm sorry." Martin hung his head. "But I was just trying to help. Your ex-wife said... Well, I guess it doesn't matter what she said, does it?"

Grady shook his head and hoisted a wide-awake Andy a little higher on his shoulder. "What happened to the original test results?"

"I kept them. In fact, I can show them to you now." Martin disappeared into the file room. He returned with a document that had been filed under *Fikleman, Clarissa.* Martin handed it over to Grady and Jenna for their perusal. "Andy is the child of Grady Noland and Jenna Sullivan."

The clatter of high heels had them all looking up. Clarissa stood in the doorway, her white mink thrown over her shoulder, her discreetly colored blond hair shining in the fluorescent light of the hospital lab. "Hello, Grady," she said in a throaty voice. She took in the furious look on Grady's face, the baby in his arms and sighed. "I guess I owe you an explanation."

"As well as an apology," Jenna said tightly.

"I wanted another try at our marriage," Clarissa said simply.

"So you produced fake documents and sworn affidavits and coerced a lab tech to switch the results of the blood tests?" Jenna asked incredulously, moving closer to Andy and Grady.

"When I did all that, I didn't think Andy was your baby, either," Clarissa said.

"It was still a lie," Jenna emphasized bluntly.

Clarissa regarded the group gathered in the Philadelphia General lab unapologetically. Her gaze sharpened as she surveyed Grady. Resignation filled her eyes. "It's futile, isn't it? You don't love me. You never did."

Grady didn't know what to say to that. Finally, he shrugged. "Maybe in the beginning..."

"But not anymore." Clarissa frowned and released a short, impatient breath. "I suppose it's just as well, because in the midst of all this, I realized something, too, Grady. You're not what I want, either. You never were." She turned on her heel and left the lab. And Grady knew that it truly was over. He was free.

JENNA ALLOWED GRADY to take her and Andy to his apartment for the night. She fed and changed Andy and settled him down in his crib for a nap while Grady put on a pot of coffee. He poured them each a cup, laced both liberally with Kahlua and topped them with generous dollops of whipped cream.

Jenna wrapped both hands around her mug and tried not to feel too cozy, sitting there with Grady at his kitchen table.

"Well, where do we go from here?" Grady asked bluntly, studying her over the rim of his cup.

Jenna shrugged, painfully aware that if not for Andy asleep in the crib nearby, she wouldn't be here with Grady at all. She drew a stabilizing breath. "I guess we decide custody of Andy. I'm willing to take full custody but—" she took another deep breath, drawing on all her courage as she attempted to be as fair as she could about this "—I'm willing to grant you liberal visitation rights."

Grady's slate-blue eyes gleamed with a mixture of displeasure and disappointment. "I don't want to visit my son. I want him with me all the time." He squeezed her hand possessively. "And I want you with me, too."

As if it was that simple. Jenna withdrew her hand from his and tried not to be too hurt Grady had put his proposition to her so bluntly. But it was an impossible task, because she *was* hurt. She had wanted hearts and flowers, declarations of wild, impassioned love. Not this matter-of-fact discussion. "How romantic of you, Grady."

Grady leaned back in his chair and kept his eyes on hers. "I'm serious," he said softly. "Why should we have to split up Andy's care? Why can't we just get married?"

Jenna gripped the handle of her stoneware mug tightly and forced herself to take a sip of the rich coffee. The scalding hot liquid didn't burn nearly as much as Grady's unromantic proposal. "Because cops and marriage don't mix, remember?" she retorted lightly, fighting for serenity.

"Marriage to a cop and Clarissa didn't mix," Grady corrected. He leaned toward her again and traced a lazy pattern on the back of her wrist. "I have a feeling you're independent and understanding enough to make a damn good cop's wife. Besides that, we're compatible—sexually and otherwise, from similar backgrounds, with a bent for public service. We share a baby."

He talked like he was stating a business case, Jenna realized miserably.

"What more could either of us want?" Grady finished pragmatically, clearly not understanding her reluctance to be with him.

How about a love that was every bit as strong and abiding as their physical passion for one another, Jenna thought miserably. How about a commitment that had nothing to do with the child they had made and everything to do with their deep feelings for one another?

"I've got a question for you, Grady," Jenna said casually, pulling her tingling wrist out of reach, "that just may help put things in perspective for you." For both of us, she thought.

He got up, went to the cupboard and returned with a bag of chocolate-chip macadamia-nut cookies. "Ask away," he said as he sat down.

"What would have happened had I not been able to prove to you beyond a shadow of a doubt that the baby I had was yours? I mean, what if we hadn't had access to DNA tests or the results of those tests had stayed screwed up or maybe just been inconclusive, then what?"

Grady offered her a cookie. She refused.

He shot her a baffled look. "What does it matter? What does any of that speculation—and that's all it is, Jenna, speculation—have to do with me asking you to marry me?"

"Is that what you just did?"

Grady released a short, impatient breath and gave her a look that said she was making this unnecessarily hard on them both. "You know I did," he said gruffly.

"Just as I also know you haven't yet answered my question, and I want an answer, Grady. What if I hadn't proved Andy was our child? What would you have done?" Could he have followed his heart, trusted in her and his love for her and realized the truth anyway?

Grady munched on a cookie and thought about it for a moment. Finally, he shrugged, as if it no longer mattered much to him either way. "Relied on Nanny Beth's eyewitness testimony to the birth, I guess."

He was being deliberately obtuse, and it infuriated her. She needed him to tell her that he would have trusted her and loved her no matter what, before she could commit to him. Being careful to keep her voice down lest they wake the sleeping Andy, Jenna said, "You're a cop, Grady. You rely on the facts, as you reminded me dozens of times this week. Would you have felt comfortable with that? Knowing you had nothing to back it up with except my word and Nanny Beth's?"

Grady shrugged. "Not as comfortable as now, no, but—"

So he didn't really trust her or love her after all, Jenna realized sadly. She got up so abruptly she jarred the table and sloshed coffee from her mug. "That's all I needed to hear." As she had the last time she had been in his Philadelphia apartment, Jenna began gathering up Andy's things. "No, I will not marry you, Grady. Yes, you can be Andy's father."

"How generous of you," Grady retorted furiously, pushing the words through his teeth. "But I don't want just a son. I want my baby and a wife."

A wife, or a glorified baby-sitter cum mistress? Jenna wondered darkly. Fury engulfed her as she thought about the way he was using her. Whether he was conscious of it or not didn't seem to matter. "My second point," Jenna said coolly. "You wouldn't be marrying me now if it weren't for Andy. And that's just not good enough, Detective!"

Looking exasperated beyond belief, Grady propped his hands on his hips and regarded Jenna sternly. "Then what would be?" he demanded.

"That's just it, Grady," Jenna told him sadly, wishing with all her heart that things were different but suspecting sadly that they never would be. "You just don't know."

Chapter Thirteen

"I know we got off to a rocky start, and that's my fault as much as Jenna's, but I thought I'd made that up to her," Grady confided dispiritedly to the three other men seated around the table in the Albany bar. "For a while, of course, we had the baby business standing in the way of our getting together, but the minute that got cleared up, I asked her to marry me, so I could be a proper husband to her and a father to Andy."

"And?" Lamar Sullivan asked, leaning forward on the edge of his chair as he waited for Grady's reply.

"And she acted like I'd just sold her a worthless piece of swampland in Florida," Grady admitted with a beleaguered sigh. "Maybe I'm being uncommonly dense here, but I don't understand why she said no, guys, and that's why I asked you all here tonight. We all love Jenna. We all care about her. I figured if we put our heads together, we might be able to shed some light on Jenna's fury with me."

"I take it that means Jenna is still refusing to take your calls," Lamar Sullivan said with an understanding sigh.

"Won't take my calls. Won't see me, period," Grady muttered as he loosened his tie with a jerk.

"Have you tried writing her a letter?" Steve Jackson asked helpfully before he popped a shelled peanut in his mouth.

"Yes. According to Nanny Beth, she won't even open the envelopes if she sees my names on the outside," Grady retorted humorlessly.

"It's only been four days," Kip said as he took a handful of pretzels from the bowl in the center of the table.

"The longest four days of my life." Grady scowled. He couldn't ever recall feeling more miserable or alone, which was why he had called this impromptu session with all the men in Jenna's life. Someone had to have a clue what to do next. God knew he was at his wit's end.

"Jenna always was high-strung," her brother admitted with a shrug. "Furthermore, when it comes to matters of the heart, she's never been all that rational."

Lamar's expression sobered sympathetically. "Give her time, Grady, she'll come around," he said.

"What if she doesn't change her mind?" Grady stared into his beer. Too late, he realized he should have believed in Jenna from the very beginning. The fact he hadn't was doubtless contributing to her anger and distrust of him now.

"It's up to you to see that she does agree to marry you, son," Lamar Sullivan said sternly. He had to strain to be heard above the jukebox.

"Any ideas how I might accomplish that?" Grady searched the faces of the men around him.

"Tried telling her you're sorry?" Kip asked.

"Yes," Grady admitted tightly as a fresh wave of frustration washed through him. *In a roundabout way.*

"And?" Every eye was glued to his face.

Grady shrugged. "She doesn't seem to want to forget and forgive."

"Maybe you're just not convincing enough," Steve Jackson speculated thoughtfully.

"I agree," Kip said. Everyone turned to look at him, including Grady. "Jenna's a woman with a lot of heart. Seems to me she wants a man with the same." Kip leveled a stern glance at Grady. "If you haven't got that, my friend, as much as we'd like you to be part of our family, you haven't got a chance."

JENNA FINISHED TYPING the letter to the United States Embassy in Budapest, urging the speedy release of the fifteen orphans who were waiting to be adopted by their Foundation parents. Her mood still grim, she printed the letter, folded it and slid it into the envelope. The doorbell rang just as she was turning off her computer.

"Jenna, darling, can you get the door?" Nanny Beth called from the second floor. "I'm in the middle of giving Andy his bath."

"No problem," Jenna called up the stairs, her mood nowhere near as pleasant as her voice. The last few days had been hell.

She trudged to the door, looked through the viewer and frowned even more. Grady Noland. Again. Would the man never give up? "Go away, Grady," she said through the door of the farmhouse.

"You said I could see my son whenever I wanted," he said.

Jenna paused. She had promised that, damn it. And damn him for reminding her. "You're supposed to call first," she said.

"I did. Nanny Beth said it was okay."

Jenna frowned. Nanny Beth had been given strict instructions that Grady was to visit Andy only when Jenna wasn't around to see him, too.

She opened the door and ushered him in. "We're going to have to talk about this."

"I agree." Grady shrugged out of his overcoat and handed it to her. "Hudson Falls is a heck of a long drive from Philadelphia. I can't keep doing this every day."

Jenna hung his coat on the rack next to the stairs. "So borrow Alec's jet."

"Very funny."

Suddenly, he was right behind her. Close enough that she could smell the spicy, masculine scent of his aftershave. Close enough that she could feel the warmth of his tall body. Pushing the memory of the passion they had shared from her mind, she turned to face him. "Andy is upstairs with Nanny Beth."

He braced a hand on the banister beside her. "I didn't come here to see Andy," he said quietly, stepping closer and invading her space, his voice so quiet she had to strain to hear him. "I came to see you."

Jenna swallowed and stepped away. Much more of his closeness and she'd end up in his arms. "We've already said everything we have to say."

"Mmm, I don't think so."

The new determination in his tone had her pulse jumping. Without warning, Nanny Beth appeared at the head of the stairs. Andy was wrapped snugly in a thick warm terry-cloth baby towel. "I thought I heard you, Grady," she said cheerfully.

Jenna glared at Nanny Beth and Grady suspiciously. "Since when did the two of you get so chummy?" she asked as Nanny Beth came down the stairs with Andy in her arms.

"Since I told her I asked you to marry me," Grady said.

"Then you also should have told her I refused your oh-so-romantic offer," Jenna snapped back. She wished she had known Grady was coming. If she had known, she would have changed out of the snug worn jeans, white turtleneck and oversize denim workshirt and into something coolly aloof and intimidating. She would have done something with her hair, pinned it back severely or something, instead of leaving it down to flow over her shoulders in soft waves.

Grady grinned and looked at Nanny Beth. "I told you she was feisty, didn't I?"

"Always been that way, probably always will be," Nanny Beth agreed. She handed Andy over to Grady. "Want to see your papa for a moment, sugar?" she asked. Andy beamed at Grady and gurgled with delight.

Jenna stared at Nanny Beth. "Whose side are you on?" she demanded.

"Yours, of course," Nanny Beth said, unperturbed, "which is why I think you should go out with Grady tonight."

"I'll go out with Grady Noland when hell freezes over. Now if you two matchmakers will excuse me, I have more work to do."

"Jenna, it's eight o'clock at night," Grady reminded.

"So?" She was so furious with him, so hurt for the nonchalant way he had proposed to her.

As quick as one-two-three, Grady handed Andy to Nanny Beth, cut Jenna off at the door to her office and threw an arm out to block out her way. "So, I think you can spare a few hours for me," he drawled, his smile so wicked it made her heart race.

Don't give in to him. Don't let him break your heart again. "Then you think wrong." Jenna ducked beneath his outstretched arm and charged into her office.

He followed her, then turned to Nanny Beth. "You're all set for tonight?" he asked her.

"Andy and I are fine," Nanny Beth said, just as mysteriously. She made a shooing motion with her free hand. "You two run along and have fun."

Jenna released an impatient sigh. Why was it that absolutely no one was listening to her this evening? "I told you, I am not going anywhere with this louse," Jenna said.

"Damn, but I love it when you're feisty," Grady said.

The next thing Jenna knew, he had closed the distance between them and swung her up into his arms. "Grady, put me down!" Jenna commanded icily.

"Gladly, as soon as we reach the limo," Grady replied. He strode past Nanny Beth with a cheerful, determined smile. "Don't wait up."

"Have a good time, darlings," Nanny Beth said with a wave.

There really was a limo outside, Jenna noted with disbelief. A white stretch limo with darkened glass and a driver who got out to open the door for Grady. "You know, Detective Noland, this is against the law," Jenna muttered as he dropped her gently onto the seat, then followed her into the car.

"Taking a woman on a date?" Grady asked innocently.

"Kidnapping a woman on a date," Jenna corrected as she started to scramble for the other side.

He made a scoffing sound and pulled her beside him. "I'm not kidnapping you."

"Are, too," Jenna insisted as the car took off and rolled smoothly down the drive to the road.

"Am not!"

They glared at one another. Jenna decided it would be undignified to struggle anymore. She would just let him say what he had to say, tell him no again, that she would not marry him, and then be done with him. She folded her arms beneath her breasts. "Okay, spit it out, Detective. Let's get this over with."

"First, open your present," Grady said.

Jenna reluctantly took the large ribbon-wrapped box he handed her only because she didn't want to prolong the argument. Inside was a beautiful red dress worthy of any screen siren. It was just her size, made by a designer she loved. Nanny Beth had to have helped him. Jenna pretended not to understand. "This is a little large for Andy," she said.

Grady threw back his head and roared with laughter. "You break me up," he said, slapping his knee.

Jenna felt a new wave of color come into her cheeks. "Right," she said dryly. She tapped a sneakered foot impatiently. "Are you done?"

"No, as a matter of fact, Ms. Jenna Sullivan, I am not." Grady reached across the seat, picked up a fragrant bouquet of red roses, and tossed the flowers in her arms. "These are for you, too."

Jenna cradled the flowers loosely in her lap. She told herself sternly that it was far too late for Grady to be behaving like the hopelessly ardent suitor she had always yearned for. No matter how many gifts he gave her, it wasn't going to do him any good. He wasn't going to be able to buy his way into her good graces. Nevertheless, without warning, she was feeling ridiculously close to tears. Getting a tight grip on her composure, she said in a harsh staccato voice, "Now are you finished?"

"Nope." Grady punched a button so that the car was filled with beautiful music and handed her another ribbon-wrapped box. Figuring she'd save them both a lot of time and energy if she just opened it—which didn't mean she had to accept the gift—Jenna tore off the ribbon. Inside was a big bottle of her favorite perfume. She knew exactly how much it cost, and he'd spent a mint on it. "I hate to tell you this, Grady, but my affections can't be bought," Jenna said dryly.

Grady ignored that and met her eyes. "How about won, then?" he said softly, so softly her heart skipped a beat.

The limo stopped in front of a popular bed-and-breakfast inn. The driver opened the door for them. Grady got out and extended a hand to her. "I don't care what else you have planned for me, I am not going to let you seduce me," Jenna whispered sternly in his ear as they started up the steps.

"I don't want to seduce you, not ever again," Grady said softly, so only she could hear. His hand tightened on hers as he ushered her through the front door of the quaint country inn. "If you come to me again, it's not going to be a reckless impulse, Jenna."

She turned to face him as she slipped inside. "Then what is it going to be?" she replied, "if not an impulse?" Until now that was the only way they had made love.

He caught her hand and tugged her close. They collided, softness to hardness, as he looked hotly down at her and teased, "You admit there's a chance for us, then?"

"I admit no such thing," Jenna said stiffly, stepping promptly away from him, but she knew he had just made his point, that deep inside she was already simmering with possibilities.

He had certainly gone to an awful lot of trouble here. Trouble that had very little to do with the baby they had made and everything to do with her, Jenna realized as she looked at the huge antique table and saw it had been set just for two. A fire was flickering warmly. Soft romantic music played in the background. The proprietress came out to meet them. "Just let us know when you're ready for the meal, Mr. Noland," she said with a charming smile. "The champagne is on ice. And the room upstairs is ready, too."

"Thank you," Grady said. Giving Jenna no chance to say a word, he ushered her toward the stairs.

Jenna told herself she was only continuing to go along with him for the pleasure of turning him down once again. "You're wasting your time here, Grady," Jenna said under her breath.

He touched a light hand to her back and guided her into the first bedroom on the right. "I'll be the judge of that."

The room was lovely, the bed a huge old four-poster, complete with canopy, lacy white comforter and crisp white sheets. Another enticing fire roared in the grate. Jenna saw a sexy red lingerie set in the same shade as the dress he'd given her in the car and carried up in the box. An old-fashioned tub stood in the corner. Grady went straight to it, turned on the water and poured a liberal amount of perfumed bubble bath under the spigot. "I'll be waiting for you downstairs," he said with another wicked smile. "Take your time. We've got all night, thanks to Nanny Beth."

I might as well be incredibly beautiful when I turn him down, Jenna thought. She locked the door after him, and then turned to the bath. It had been a long time since she'd been pampered, a long time since she'd been alone with Grady. Five whole days, in fact, since they'd spent any time together at all....

When she walked downstairs, he was waiting for her, dressed not in the casual clothing he had worn to pick her up, but in a tux. He looked freshly showered and shaved. Jenna felt her heart skip another beat. Maybe it wasn't going to be as easy to say no to him tonight as she'd thought.

"Champagne?" He got up to pour them both a drink.

Jenna struggled to contain her euphoria. "It's not going to work," she told him again. She looked around, hoping for any distraction. "And where is the proprietress?"

"Upstairs in her private quarters. I told her I'd summon her if we needed her, but I don't expect to need her."

For the first time, Jenna noted the covered silver chafing dishes on the sideboard. Their dinner, no doubt. "Where are the other guests?" And why was her heart suddenly pounding so?

Grady stood in front of the fireplace. "There aren't any tonight. I rented out the whole inn."

He had a trust fund, she reminded herself. So even if this was costing him a mint, it wasn't as if he wouldn't eat lunch for a month because of his extravagance. Money didn't matter to him anyway, any more than it mattered to her. She met his eyes. "Why?"

"That should be obvious."

She remained on the other side of the mantel. "It's not," Jenna said stubbornly. He hadn't made it easy for her, and she wasn't going to make it easy for him.

He crossed to her side, stepped behind her and wrapped his arms around her. "Because tonight is the most important night of our lives," he whispered against her hair.

Jenna leaned against the solid warmth of his chest just for a moment. She closed her eyes and tried not to think of how much she still longed to hold him and make love to him again. "I don't know how you can say that," she said thickly, knowing that as much as she loved him—and she did love Grady Noland deeply—

she never wanted to be the wife he'd had to marry because of the baby they'd made.

Grady pressed a kiss in her hair and turned her gently to face him. One arm slid around her back, holding her close. The other hand cupped her chin and guided her face up to his. "I say it because it's true," he said, all the tenderness she had ever dreamed of radiating in his low, sexy voice. His slate-blue eyes roved her upturned features. "I screwed up before, Jenna," he confessed miserably. "I thought I was being sensible, limiting myself to casual affairs, refusing to even consider marriage."

"And then Andy changed all that," Jenna interrupted sadly. Andy. Not her.

"No, Jenna," Grady corrected sternly as he tightened his possessive grip on her waist, "*you* changed all that. From the night I met you there's never been anyone else." He bent and touched his lips lightly to hers. "Nor will there ever be again."

Tears glistened in her eyes but did not fall. Her mouth trembled with the emotions that had caused her to run from his cookies-and-coffee proposal in the first place. "You're just saying that because you want the baby," she accused.

Grady shook his head. His eyes were dark, intense. "I'm saying it because I want you. I know I wasn't romantic enough before, Jenna, and I'm sorry for that, so sorry."

Jenna shook her head in silent censure as she stepped from the warm, inviting circle of his arms. "My turning you down had nothing to do with your lack of romantic notions, Grady. In fact, romance per se can be just as deceptive as the cold, hard facts."

"Then let me tell you what's in my heart," Grady said gruffly. He tugged a chair close with his foot, sank down into it and pulled her onto his lap. "I love you, Jenna." He held her tenderly, looking deep into her eyes. "I have always loved you. Even when your actions and mine made no sense, I loved you," he said softly.

Jenna's spirits soared. Her heart did cartwheels in her chest. She wrapped her arms about his neck and pulled him closer still. "Those are feelings you're talking about now, Grady," Jenna teased.

"I know."

Jenna paused, her fingertips resting on the starched collar of his pleated white shirt. "Are you sure you can trust them?" she asked tremulously.

"Yes," Grady said softly, firmly. "I am. And you know why? Because those feelings I have in my heart will never change. I'm always going to love you, Jenna. Whether we share a baby or not, whether you wear my wedding ring or not, I will still love you."

"That's all I needed to hear." Jenna tugged him closer, and they indulged in a long, steamy kiss that left her feeling glowing and alive.

"Better?" Grady asked, when at last they drew apart.

"Better," Jenna confided in a shaky voice. She paused as she looked at him again. "But why didn't you just tell me that back at the farmhouse?" she asked softly. "Why did you go to all this trouble?" Surely he knew he didn't have to. All she had ever wanted to know was that he loved her and wanted to marry him, baby or no baby.

Grady gave her a very smug, very male smile. "Because I wanted us to celebrate the Valentine's Day we never had, the way we should have in the first place, the way we will every year from now on," he said.

"Flowers and everything?" Jenna teased.

"Flowers, tux, sexy new red dress and everything," Grady affirmed. "I never thought I'd actually be saying this, or feeling this, but..." He shook his head as if he couldn't quite believe it. "You bring out the romantic in me, Jenna."

Jenna laughed, delighted. "And you bring out the romantic in me," she confided, lifting her mouth to his.

Grady kissed her again, deeply, lingeringly, until she was limp with surrender, tingling with longing. "Is that a yes?" he said. "Will you marry me?"

Jenna smiled up at him, knowing all was right with their world at last. "Yes, Grady," she said. "I will."

INDULGE A LITTLE 6947 SWEEPSTAKES
NO PURCHASE NECESSARY

HERE'S HOW THE SWEEPSTAKES WORKS:
The Harlequin Reader Service shipments for January, February and March 1994 will contain, respectively, coupons for entry into three prize drawings: a trip for two to San Francisco, an Alaskan cruise for two and a trip for two to Hawaii. To be eligible for any drawing using an Entry Coupon, simply complete and mail according to directions.

There is no obligation to continue as a Reader Service subscriber to enter and be eligible for any prize drawing. You may also enter any drawing by hand printing your name and address on a 3" x 5" card and the destination of the prize you wish that entry to be considered for (i.e., San Francisco trip, Alaskan cruise or Hawaiian trip). Send your 3" x 5" entries to: Indulge a Little 6947 Sweepstakes, c/o Prize Destination you wish that entry to be considered for, P.O. Box 1315, Buffalo, NY 14269-1315, U.S.A. or Indulge a Little 6947 Sweepstakes, P.O. Box 610, Fort Erie, Ontario L2A 5X3, Canada.

To be eligible for the San Francisco trip, entries must be received by 4/30/94; for the Alaskan cruise, 5/31/94; and the Hawaiian trip, 6/30/94. No responsibility is assumed for lost, late or misdirected mail. Sweepstakes open to residents of the U.S. (except Puerto Rico) and Canada, 18 years of age or older. All applicable laws and regulations apply. Sweepstakes void wherever prohibited.

For a copy of the Official Rules, send a self-addressed, stamped envelope (WA residents need not affix return postage) to: Indulge a Little 6947 Rules, P.O. Box 4631, Blair, NE 68009, U.S.A.

INDR93

INDULGE A LITTLE 6947 SWEEPSTAKES
NO PURCHASE NECESSARY

HERE'S HOW THE SWEEPSTAKES WORKS:
The Harlequin Reader Service shipments for January, February and March 1994 will contain, respectively, coupons for entry into three prize drawings: a trip for two to San Francisco, an Alaskan cruise for two and a trip for two to Hawaii. To be eligible for any drawing using an Entry Coupon, simply complete and mail according to directions.

There is no obligation to continue as a Reader Service subscriber to enter and be eligible for any prize drawing. You may also enter any drawing by hand printing your name and address on a 3" x 5" card and the destination of the prize you wish that entry to be considered for (i.e., San Francisco trip, Alaskan cruise or Hawaiian trip). Send your 3" x 5" entries to: Indulge a Little 6947 Sweepstakes, c/o Prize Destination you wish that entry to be considered for, P.O. Box 1315, Buffalo, NY 14269-1315, U.S.A. or Indulge a Little 6947 Sweepstakes, P.O. Box 610, Fort Erie, Ontario L2A 5X3, Canada.

To be eligible for the San Francisco trip, entries must be received by 4/30/94; for the Alaskan cruise, 5/31/94; and the Hawaiian trip, 6/30/94. No responsibility is assumed for lost, late or misdirected mail. Sweepstakes open to residents of the U.S. (except Puerto Rico) and Canada, 18 years of age or older. All applicable laws and regulations apply. Sweepstakes void wherever prohibited.

For a copy of the Official Rules, send a self-addressed, stamped envelope (WA residents need not affix return postage) to: Indulge a Little 6947 Rules, P.O. Box 4631, Blair, NE 68009, U.S.A.

INDR93

INDULGE A LITTLE

SWEEPSTAKES

OFFICIAL ENTRY COUPON

This entry must be received by: APRIL 30, 1994
This month's winner will be notified by: MAY 15, 1994
Trip must be taken between: JUNE 30, 1994-JUNE 30, 1995

YES, I want to win the San Francisco vacation for two. I understand that the prize includes round-trip airfare, first-class hotel, rental car and pocket money as revealed on the "wallet" scratch-off card.

Name____________________

Address ____________ Apt. ________

City____________________

State/Prov.__________ Zip/Postal Code________

Daytime phone number________________
(Area Code)

Account #____________________

Return entries with invoice in envelope provided. Each book in this shipment has two entry coupons—and the more coupons you enter, the better your chances of winning!

 MONTH1

INDULGE A LITTLE

SWEEPSTAKES

OFFICIAL ENTRY COUPON

This entry must be received by: APRIL 30, 1994
This month's winner will be notified by: MAY 15, 1994
Trip must be taken between: JUNE 30, 1994-JUNE 30, 1995

YES, I want to win the San Francisco vacation for two. I understand that the prize includes round-trip airfare, first-class hotel, rental car and pocket money as revealed on the "wallet" scratch-off card.

Name____________________

Address ____________ Apt. ________

City____________________

State/Prov.__________ Zip/Postal Code________

Daytime phone number________________
(Area Code)

Account #____________________

Return entries with invoice in envelope provided. Each book in this shipment has two entry coupons—and the more coupons you enter, the better your chances of winning!

© 1993 HARLEQUIN ENTERPRISES LTD. MONTH1